For my wife.

broken

Susan Jane Bigelow

Candlemark & Gleam

First trade paperback edition published 2011.

This is a work of fiction. Names, characters, places, and incidents
either are the product of the author's imagination or are used
fictitiously. Any resemblance to actual events, locales, or persons,
living or dead, is entirely coincidental.

For information, address
Candlemark & Gleam LLC,
104 Morgan Street, Bennington, VT 05201
info@candlemarkandgleam.com

Library of Congress Cataloging-in-Publication Data
In Progress

ISBN: 978-1-936460-04-5

Cover art and design by Kate Sullivan

Book design and composition by Kate Sullivan
Typeface: Candara

Editors: Kate Sullivan and Vivien Weaver
Proofreader: Laura Duncan

www.candlemarkandgleam.com

[PROLOGUE]

To be opened by Michael Forward
November 10th, 2106

Hello, Michael,

You don't know me, but I knew Joe very well. He and I were good friends when I lived on Earth. By the time you get this letter, I'll have been dead for several years. However, since I possess the same sorts of abilities you and Joe both have, I am able to know when you will need it, and I've arranged to have it sent to you then.

You've seen her in your mind many times, the woman with the baby in the subway station. You have some idea of what the baby could mean.

The train is the 10:14 Silver westbound, at the

Union Tower station, platform 2. The date, you know already.

I won't tell you that it's important. You know that, too.

Try to find Silverwyng — she will help you. Ask at Union Tower.

I'm sorry. Please know that. And thank you.

All of my love,

VAL

Valentino Altrera
West Arve, Valen, Terran Confederation
August 4th, 2101

[CHAPTER 1]

BROKEN REMEMBERED FLIGHT.
She lay on her back, belly aching with hunger. Nearby, a space-bound ship heaved itself off the ground with a sigh and a groan, then sluggishly powered its way up towards the outer atmosphere and the vacuum beyond.

<>► ◄<>

She followed its path with her finger, tracing the dissipating wake back and forth. Silverwyng had been more graceful by far.

<>► ◄<>

Her stomach howled in pain. She groggily stood and staggered off towards the nearest place she knew of where she could get something to eat.

Broken remembered the rush of wind against her cheeks, whipping her long hair out behind her in a flashing silver arc.

The mission looked like any other: Third Perthist Universalist Ministries. It was in the dark, dingy basement of a building standing in a neighborhood that had never quite been rebuilt since the war. The Sisters there gave Broken the eye; they knew her.

"Have you been drinking again?" one asked, fixing her with a disapproving stare. Broken didn't say anything. Her head hurt. One downside to being her was that it took an awful lot of booze to get really drunk. She usually ran out of money first.

They gave her a plate of greasy something and a slice of something else. It may have been cheese, but Broken couldn't really see it too well. She ate it anyway, and immediately felt better. Her system needed to recharge. She mumbled her thanks and shuffled outside. She'd come back again when she got hungry enough. She always did.

A tall, brilliantly handsome man took her hand as they leapt into the night sky together. Her heart soared.

She poked through some garbage cans, looking for anything she could use or sell. Jude would buy pretty much anything, if it didn't stink too badly. Eventually she gave up and settled in an alley next to a trash compactor, huddling desperately against its cold metal sides in a futile attempt to get warm. Winter was coming on. Maybe she ought to go south. She'd always wanted to. She might be happier if she were warm all year. She reached into her coat pocket and felt something cool and hard.

An unopened bottle of something strong. She took a rushed swallow and felt the warmth spread through her. Her eyes grew heavy. Thoughts of heading south evaporated like droplets of alcohol from her lips. She drained the entire bottle as fast as she could, and waited for oblivion.

Broken remembered...
... she couldn't stop remembering.

She jerked awake. Two men in dark, irregular uniforms with black and white armbands marked with stars loomed at the far end of the alley. Black Bands; Reform Party militia. She scrunched into a little ball. She didn't want Black Bands to notice her. They'd caught her once, and...

She moaned softly despite herself.

A shrill squeak, something animal, brought her back to her senses. They had a cat, they were...

Broken liked cats. Fury burned through her.

She stood. She was still drunk. Of all the times... She swayed back and forth dangerously before she found her legs. The two Black Bands looked her way.

"Drop the cat," she heard herself say, voice slurred and shaky. "Or else."

A beat.

That was easy! How long had it taken Silverwyng to get to this point? She'd agonized and searched her soul for months before doing this. Broken had less to lose, perhaps, than Silverwyng.

The man opened his hand. The cat hit the ground and sprinted away to safety. Their quarry lost, the Black Bands advanced on her instead. She crouched in a ridiculous fighting pose, desperately reaching back to remember some of her training as they bashed her head in.

She returned from the dead some hours later.

A red mist blanketed her field of vision. Her bones stretched and knitted themselves back together; her muscles contracted and expanded; her lip's two halves found each other, latched on, and sewed themselves up. Her body contorted and crackled, trying to piece itself back together in the time it takes to carve a turkey.

She writhed and spun in agony. Blood—hers—had soaked through all her clothes. The pain was unbearable, excruciating.

She spat out a tooth, moaning in pain. A new

tooth was already driving its way through her gum. She laughed and screamed at the same time. Ecstasy. She loved it. She *loved* it.

[CHAPTER 2]

"EXCUSE ME," THE NERVOUS-LOOKING young man said, "But I'm looking for someone. Perhaps you can help me."

The secretary looked up from her screen, where she had been reading a fine novel of highest-class erotica, and sighed, looking him up and down. He was small and slight, skinny like a boy, but with anxious, intelligent eyes and a strange, pinched expression on his face. He was trying not to look at her. "Yeah?"

"Her name is—was—Silverwyng. Spelled with a 'y' in the 'wyng,' I believe. I know that she lived here, once."

The secretary sighed again, this time with more flair; she had a whole repertoire of sighs for annoying visitors. "We don't give out personal information about Union members."

"I'm a reporter." He gave her a complicated ID card; she took her time swiping it. "I work for the *Reformist Monthly*, I've been assigned to profile some lesser-known Union members. Is there anyone I can talk to?"

The secretary spent several resentful, unhurried minutes scanning through his credentials, but at last tapped a message into her computer. The *Reformist Monthly* sounded too official to ignore completely. "Mr., uh, Forward, Sky Ranger is going to come down and see you," she said. "Consider yourself lucky." It was obvious from her tone that she wished herself in his place, all of a sudden.

"Thank you," he replied courteously, trying not to shriek with anticipation. Sky Ranger! He'd had Sky Ranger posters on his wall when he was little. Joe had disapproved for some reason, but Michael hadn't cared.

He took a moment to look around. Union Tower. He'd always wanted to come here as a kid, to fly with the Union members, but he knew well enough he never would. This would be his only visit. Maybe one more, but if he had to come back here, his life would be almost over. The place was decorated like a fancy whorehouse. Gold trim, expensive paintings, marble floors... It had cost the government a fortune to build it for them.

A few minutes later, a huge man with a shock of jet-black hair, steely blue eyes and a neatly trimmed goatee strode out of the lift. *Why would Sky Ranger take the lift?* Michael wondered idly. Trying not to offend visitors? He was not dressed in his customary tan and white outfit, but instead in what looked almost like a Black Band uniform. It was mostly black, with white collar and trim, and the new Confederation flag was appliqued on the front and sleeves.

Michael Forward instantly saw about three dozen possibilities, and wished he hadn't. All except two ended in darkest tragedy. He wanted to shout at this man who had once been his hero, to grab his ears and scream, "How could you?!" into them. Was *this* why Joe hadn't liked the man? Could he see it all coming, the devastating possibilities? But Sky Ranger had done nothing yet. And so Michael could do nothing but sit back and watch the trains slam into one another. So much for heroes.

Cynicism didn't become him, Michael thought, but then, he didn't really have a choice. He'd seen hundreds of his own future possibilities, too, and he always ended up bitter and angry. If he lived that long.

"Hello, young sir!" Sky Ranger boomed. "You're a Party reporter?

"Uh, yes," Michael said. "I'm doing a piece for *Reformist Monthly*."

"Oh! Fantastic! I'm a Party member, you know," said Sky Ranger, guiding him into the lift, which was fitted with a glass capsule that looked out onto the courtyard. "A lot of my people support what the Reform Party is doing these days, and we're big fans of President Peltan." The lift shuddered and rocketed upward. Michael felt faintly ill as the ground dropped away. The effect was rather like flying, Michael supposed. That might be the point.

Sky Ranger continued. "I always have been, right from the beginning. I joined the Party early on, before President Peltan was even a senator. Great things we're doing, great things. More than just saving one life or two, but saving *everybody*, more than any of my people could ever do on their own. You see what I mean?"

The lift sighed to a halt, and they exited into a spacious office. Beauty surrounded them. The office was dominated by a huge window that looked out over much of this part of the city. Union Tower was one of the tallest buildings east of the Hudson, and Sky Ranger's office had to be near the top floor. A carved wooden desk, inlaid with intricate patterns and swirls, sat in the middle of the space. Michael, trying to look as nonchalant as he thought a Reform Party reporter would feel, took a seat and helped himself to some candy from the delicate crystal dish on the desk.

"So," said Sky Ranger. "I've probably read your publication."

"Actually, we're pretty new," said Michael evenly. "New programs and all that. But you'll be seeing a lot of us in the future." He tried to look smug.

"Even better!" Sky Ranger smiled broadly. "Now, what is it you wanted to talk to me about?"

Many things, thought Michael. But he said, "This could just be a beginning. For now, I was hoping you could help me find someone. She was a Union member once. She went by 'Silverwyng,' with a 'y'. This would have been about ten years ago."

Sky Ranger said nothing for a moment, then sat down and cupped his massive chin in his equally massive hand, crossing one leg over the other.

Jesus, even his thinking is dramatic. All part of the same show, Michael supposed.

"Hmmm...." he rumbled. "You know, I do recall a Union member going by that, a few years back. She could fly, I believe, right? Whatever happened to her?"

"I... was hoping you could tell me."

Sky Ranger laughed, but his eyes had narrowed, and his tone sharpened. "Well. She's no longer here, that I know. I don't remember much more. Let me think a minute."

He sat back in his chair and posed thoughtfully again. Michael could only marvel. Here sat a man with the strength of a Titan, who could destroy an entire city block with an errant mental flicker, the head of the Extrahuman Union, posing and strutting like a vain teenager in front of his mirror. Did he think that Michael was taking pictures?

"I have to say I can't remember what became of her," Sky Ranger said at last. "It's unusual for one of my people to leave the Tower permanently—in fact, that's illegal. As you well know." He sighed. "It was a long time ago. Around a decade, I think. We searched for her but found nothing. I promise you, if she is even still alive, she's no threat. I can have you check with our archivist, however. Fifteenth floor; there are signs. I'll tell him to expect you." Sky Ranger suddenly seemed a lot less friendly, "Why are you looking for her?"

"Orders," Michael said, shrugging.

"Ah." They sat in silence for a moment. "So. Is there anything else?"

"No," Michael said. "That's about it. For now. But I'll be back."

"All right, then." It was the end of the conversation; yet Sky Ranger still seemed embarrassingly desperate to please. "So. Put in a good word for the organization, and for my people, huh?" he said, a bit too jovially. "We need all the support we can get. Mention to the locals that I'm a loyal Party guy?"

Michael glanced at Sky Ranger's cold blue eyes and had a sudden vision of the Union's leader asking his secretary to run a background check on Michael and *Reformist Monthly*. Just in case. Right; he didn't have much time, then.

"Will do," said Michael cautiously.

"Great! Strength, then!"

"Honor," Michael intoned, giving a traditional Reformist reply. He found his way out of the glorious, light-filled office, and back into the lift. Fifteenth floor.

An old man wearing several Reformist pins sat behind an ancient computer terminal, absently clicking through page after page of Union reports.

Michael had a sudden vision of the old man gingerly planting a small, heavy device on an exposed beam of the Tower, pressing a button, and then, sadly, sitting on the ground to wait. Michael shook it off.

Michael explained himself, and the stooped old man's eyes lit up.

"There are many loyal Reformists here," he said. "Myself among them."

"...I'm glad to hear that. I'll remember it," Michael promised. That seemed to be what he wanted to hear.

"Did they give you anything for me?"

What? "Uh, no. Not this time."

The old man nodded. "I see. You wanted...?"

Michael explained about Silverwyng. The old archivist made a face.

"Hnng... I remember her. Yes, that was about ten years ago, was it not? She's not here, now. She left. Illegal." He coughed into a handkerchief. When had Michael last seen a handkerchief? "Let me see..." He tapped a few commands into his terminal, then swiveled the screen around so Michael could see.

A short scene looped endlessly; Sky Ranger, in his tan and white outfit, black hair gloriously perfect, perched atop the Tower's curved peak, cape swirling in the breeze. A thin young woman with striking silver hair, dressed in a feminine version of Sky Ranger's uniform, alighted next to him. Their eyes locked, she smiled, their lips met. The recording looped back, and the scene played again.

A shock ran through Michael. She had been that close to Sky Ranger? He had seemed to not even remember her.

She seemed very happy and confident, and difficult to forget. He thought of the shattered, filthy woman with the heavy eyes he saw in his visions as Silverwyng once again landed next to Sky Ranger, smiled and kissed him, blissfully unaware of what the future held.

"Who was she? What happened to her?"

The archivist sighed, a heavy rasp. "Was a member of the Union's Law Enforcement Division. That's the uniform they're wearing, of course. Flyer, self-healer. Stopped being able to fly, though, just before she left us. Broke her heart." He jabbed at the image of Sky Ranger on the screen. "*He* forgot all about her. Sad story."

"Oh," said Michael quickly. His time was short. "So where did she go?"

The old archivist sifted through his records. "Left the Union. Lessee. Last known location... somewhere in the city. No beacon. Highly irregular. There was a hunt, but it didn't turn up anything. Can't tell you any more than that."

Crap. Some possible futures had the old man giving him somewhere to check.

"I need something specific," he insisted, hoping for more. "Reform Party business." *Come on. I have no time.*

The old man's eyes narrowed. "I'm sorry." He shook his head. "If you want to find her that badly, the last track we had of her was a few years back in the Bronx. A Perthist shelter reported a Healer to us."

"Address?" Michael did his best to sound authoritarian. It worked.

"Third Perthist Ministries in the Bronx," the old man grumbled. "I can't give you any more."

"You've been most helpful," said Michael.

A message flashed on the archivist's screen. *Time's up,* thought Michael.

The old man turned the screen away from Michael, read it, and looked back up angrily.

"Hey, you—!" he started. But Michael had already gone.

[CHAPTER 3]

WINTER HAD SETTLED THICKLY AND
suddenly on the endless city. Michael walked quickly
away from the Union Tower. He dared a glance back up
to the top, where he could just make out the silhouette
of a man against the sky. Sky Ranger was out looking
for him. He darted into the nearby subway station. He
checked a mirror, and watched his own possibilities spi-
ral out of it into his mind; Sky Ranger wouldn't find him
this time. Next time he probably would.

He checked his watch. Plenty of time. It had been
stupid to go to Union Tower first, but in the end it had
worked out. Okay.

A nauseating sense of déjà vu washed over him.
He'd been here a hundred, a thousand times before,
looking in the mirror. The subway, the woman, the baby.

Now, at last, he was here for real. If the letter could

be trusted. His heart pounded as he walked slowly down to the platform. Commuters and travelers lounged near the tracks, waiting.

He'd almost burned the letter, along with just about everything else, after Joe died, but for some reason, at the last moment, he'd snatched it from the fire.

This was the moment Valentino Altrera had wanted him for. The letter he had sent seemed heavy in Michael's inside jacket pocket.

Joe had believed in Altrera; they'd been very close once. Val, Joe had said, was like them. He could see things that might, or would, happen in the future. He was *strong*, maybe the greatest prescient ever. Joe had followed Altrera when the great prophet had lived in Hartford with a small band of disciples. Altrera had later taken most of his followers to Valen, a world that now bore his name, leaving Joe behind. Even from light-years away, he'd still had a hold over Joe that Michael had often found difficult to fathom.

Part of him wanted to do what Val Altrera asked. It would make Joe proud. But another part of him wanted to run away, as fast and as far as possible.

He breathed in and out. Staying in place was easy. *Breathe.* Breathe. Wait. Stay.

Look up.

Here she comes.

She was about thirty, but looked older. She had ratty black hair, and a big bruise on her cheek. He saw nothing but a yawning black chasm when he looked at her.

He tried to shut it out, and fought down the impulse to run away. He could feel his feet start to move.

Too late—she made straight for him.

This was it, then. No more waiting.

His heart pounded. His possibilities all had this moment, but he didn't have to take it. He could put it down. He could run away. He could *live*. The world would shift and change—he felt the possibilities morphing and twisting out ahead of him. *This* moment, more than any other, could change them all.

"Take him," the woman said shakily. "*Take* him." She pressed a warm, squirming bundle into his arms.

There was no choice, really. He took it from her, and half of the possibilities winked out of existence.

He felt his hands cradle the baby close. Two shining black pearl eyes stared at him. *Oh, God, I was right.*

—*There was a man at the head of a glorious army. He brought freedom. He brought victory. He had remade the universe in his own image. Blue banners flew everywhere he went.*

—*There was a man at the head of a terrifying army. Blood spilled at his feet, the worlds bent to him. The black banners of the Reformists flew above him. His was the fist that encircled the Earth, and clenched shut.*

A thousand permutations of those two themes flew into Michael's head. So *strong*. He'd never met anyone like this.

It was too much. *I'm too young for this*, he thought desperately. He looked around. Surely someone else would take the baby? Surely he wouldn't have to.

He barely noticed that the mother had staggered

off and thrown herself in front of the 10:14. A crowd gasped. The baby began to squirm and cry.

Michael regained enough of himself to sprint up and, out of the station, before the police could stop him. He scanned the gray heavens quickly; Sky Ranger had gone.

The world seemed to waver and spin around them. Possibilities swam through the air, coming off the baby in waves. He tried to shove them out of his head.

There. He'd done it. He had no choice but to continue now, into the short, painful future that waited for him. Val's letter seemed to burn against his chest, inside his black jacket.

The baby's cries were getting more insistent. People were staring.

Michael quickly secured the baby in his pack, head poking out the top—for some reason that seemed to calm him down—and struck west. The Bronx. The bombed-out Bronx. He had to get there as soon as possible. That was where Third Perthist Ministries was.

He had to find the silver-haired woman, *now*. He remembered enough of the possibilities to realize just how much she mattered to the direction he wanted things to go.

Plus, Val Altrera had said to find her. So he would. He had to. It was that simple.

He didn't notice the two men with black armbands fall in line behind him.

Broken stretched and shook. It was colder today—

winter at last. She'd eaten something rancid, and wanted to puke it up, but couldn't let herself. She'd pass it
through; whatever bad things were in it wouldn't hurt
her. Nothing could hurt her, not really.

She hadn't been so hungry in years. Something
crawled next to her feet. A rat. Her left hand darted out
and clutched it tightly. It shrieked and squirmed and
sank its teeth into her hand, but she held on, then bit its
head off.

She ate the whole rat, bones and all. Her body
could digest anything. It would be painful, but she could
do it.

A wave of agony coursed through her, then stopped
abruptly. Her hand had healed, but she still craved food.

She knew she was a bloody wreck; they'd probably
haul her in. She didn't want the transmitter back; she'd
have to cut her arm off again. But she had to eat. She
glanced cautiously out of the alley, and spied a vendor
with a cart close by. She raced towards it, waving and
screaming.

The man was terrified enough of the crazy woman with blood caked into her hair and clothes to freeze
while she stole six hot dogs and a can of juice. She raced
back to the alley, then hid under a pile of garbage to eat.
The cops might come, they might not. If they did, they'd
take a cursory look around the alley and go.

The hot dogs were awful and cold, but they filled
her up. She felt her strength creeping back, bit by bit.
Her mind cleared.

Memory flooded her.

◆►◄◆

Doc watched her eat. "Lordy, she packs it away. I suppose she must need the energy. Did she really lose her entire hand?"

"Yeah," said Crimson Cadet (who would die only a few weeks later), shaking his head. "I've never seen anyone heal so fast. But," he lowered his voice, "she screamed the whole time. It looked like it hurt her something awful."

The food was so good, she didn't care what they said.

Broken moaned and put her hand on something soft and cold.

She risked letting a little light peek in through her eyelids, and wished she hadn't. It was the cat. The poor thing had bled to death; the Black Bands had damaged her too badly.

Despite herself, Broken started to shake uncontrollably. She didn't care if the cops found her. "Kitty," she rasped. "Kitty..."

Nothing she touched ever turned out right. She wept, sobs wracking her unwashed body, as she cradled the tiny, furry corpse.

Michael picked his way clumsily through the unfamiliar streets of New York. He'd grown up north of here, and wasn't quite sure where to begin. To make a bad situation worse, the baby, tucked into his backpack as a makeshift carrier, was starting to fuss and wail again.

Michael realized belatedly that he didn't know the

first thing about taking care of a baby. Maybe Silverw-yng would, if he ever could find her.

One possibility he *had* seen was himself and the baby wandering around New York searching for her until they froze to death. He tried not to think about that one.

Maybe the kid was hungry. Or maybe he had just filled his diaper. Come to think of it, something did smell. And the only diaper he had was the one he'd been wearing when his mother had handed him off to Michael, right before she chucked herself in front of the northbound express.

He glanced over at Union Tower, now just a thin spindle rising in the east. Sky Ranger had probably stopped looking for him. They had better things to do than chase down kids who pretended to be Reformist journalists. Didn't they?

Just in case, he tried to keep out of the way of the cops and the Black Bands.

He stopped in a grocery store and bought some diapers and bottled baby formula. Well-armed, he slipped into a convenient bathroom. When he took the kid out of the backpack, he was greeted with a terrifying stench. The kid hadn't been *wearing* a diaper, just a pair of bulky shorts. Michael had had some food in there, but he was sure he didn't want it anymore. He doubted he could salvage the backpack, since a moldering pile of baby shit now lay in the bottom.

"Aw, man," he griped as he ran the water into the pack. "Look what you did."

The baby, happy to be free of his clothes and the backpack, giggled at Michael. His coffee-brown skin looked a little raw, at least in the places where it wasn't covered by something foul. As Michael, fighting down his rising gorge, took a paper towel to the kid's behind, he felt something warm and wet trickling on his head.

The kid laughed as he peed all over the counter and floor. An older man entered the bathroom, took one look at the situation, and left quickly with a "glad that ain't me" expression on his face.

Why, Michael wondered for the millionth time, didn't his visions ever warn him of *these* sorts of possibilities?

It took nearly half an hour for Michael to clean the baby thoroughly enough so that he didn't royally stink. Maybe he wouldn't have to go for a while. Did he need some sort of ointment for the raw patches? The backpack, he cleaned as much as he could, although it still had a lingering odor. Michael got some formula down the baby (and some on the walls of the bathroom) and zipped him up in the backpack again. Mercifully, the kid fell asleep as soon as he was secure.

The sun had set over the Hudson by the time Michael made it back outside. This was getting ridiculous. He needed to find Silverwyng, *really* soon.

He glanced around. Two guys were hanging out at the corner, watching him through heavy-lidded eyes. No one else was nearby. The baby made a few "maah" noises, but stayed mostly asleep. Thank God. Michael hoisted the pack and set off towards Harlem and the Bronx beyond.

He cut through a neighborhood of small detached

houses, past three memorials to the firebombing of 2046, and found himself facing a busy expressway. He checked his map. He'd gone too far to the west, and he needed to backtrack. With a sigh, he set off southeast.

Something scampered into the shadows just inside his field of vision. Was someone following them already? He shook hishead. Nothing to be done for it. Just keep going. One foot in front of the other. Try to lose them, maybe dart down an alley.

The kid started to sniffle and cry. Weary down to his bones, Michael felt like doing the same. He'd been walking for hours, his feet were killing him, and he was hungrier than he'd been in a long time. He started to wish he'd taken the subway, even with the risks he saw in those possibilities.

He finally crossed under the expressway and entered the older part of the city. It had remained pretty much unchanged since the 2020s, when the last great urban renewal drive had taken place. No one had bothered to rebuild a lot of it after the Last War, so bomb craters and tumbledown buildings were a common sight.

She lived here, somewhere.

He was still being followed. He would look behind him every so often and see a figure trying to look nonchalant, or glancing quickly away. There were maybe five of them, now, and they were bad at this.

He knew who they were. He knew who they represented. Some of his possibilities—more than he cared to admit—began with these men and ended with him be-

fore the thin man himself, prostrate on the ground, before they shot a bolt of white-hot light through his skull.

All of those possibilities ended with the boy in
their hands, leading their armies. He hated the thought.

He slipped into an alleyway, and crawled over the
low wreck of a fence. The baby, miraculously, made not
a sound. He could hear some shifting and cursing; bums,
probably, or other night wanderers. He stole silently down
towards the river, and hid behind a trash compactor.

Two of the men sauntered too-casually into his
field of vision. He held the baby close, trying to lull him
to sleep, desperately hoping they wouldn't notice him.
This was one of those moments he'd perceived. Sometimes, they took him. Other times, he got away. When
the baby cried, they took him. If the baby stayed quiet,
they escaped. Simple, mostly.

Michael Forward held his breath. Another man, taller
than the others, joined the group. Then two more came.

The baby woke up, and his huge black eyes filled
with tears.

Shit. He covered the tiny boy's mouth with a thick
rag.

Too late. A piercing cry escaped the infant's lips,
and the men turned and pelted in Michael's direction. He
scooped the baby up in his arms and burst into a dead
run. The cries grew louder, giving their pursuers a beacon to fix on. Michael cursed. No possibilities. None. Nowhere was safe; he needed *silence!*

Suddenly, he pulled up short, almost dropping the
boy into the swirling, icy depths of the Hudson.

Dead end.

Michael fell to his knees as the men advanced.

They seemed pleased. They could finish the job tonight, instead of taking days or weeks.

Michael trembled and felt bile rising in his mouth. He'd never been so afraid. They would kill him. It was over, already. *Too soon!* he thought wildly.

"Please," he whimpered, "please..."

The men grinned. One of them drew a shiny knife. Michael could see his distorted reflection in its blade.

Possibilities. He died, over and over, his life's blood spilling on the cold ground. He would never even meet the man behind it all. He'd die in a few minutes. They would kill him now. His life was over *now.* Now. *NOW.*

Michael drew a rattling breath. The men converged, the baby cried.

"Take him," Michael said, extending his arms to the men. "Please, please, anything..." *I want to live!*

"Take him!" Michael heard himself say again. He glanced at the men, then, and knew he was damned.

They were going to take the baby, and then kill him anyway. No escape. All for nothing.

One of the men strode forward, and reached for the baby. A gurgling sound came from behind them, followed by a great heaving of water, and a wracking cough. The men, distracted for a moment, turned.

She emerged from the water, tattered clothes clinging to her sides, long silver hair plastered to her head. She strode ashore, and took in the scene.

Michael recognized her at once, and took the only chance he had.

"Silverwyng!" he cried. "*Help!*"

◄►►◄◄►

Broken had been trying to kill herself again. What else could she do, after the day she'd had? She'd chosen drowning this time, because it was much more painful and took a very long time. She'd jumped off a low bridge and fought to stay under the icy water. But this time, her heart wasn't in it. She'd just come back to life and be as miserable as ever. So she let the current bear her south, towards the sea. Maybe she'd float to Australia, or to China.

The cold numbed her, and eventually she felt like getting out. She swam to shore, and dragged herself up onto the beach.

Four men were menacing a kid and a small baby.

Staying out, she told herself forcefully. She wasn't in the LED anymore. Everything she tried to save ended up worse off than before, like the cat.

But the kid turned to her and, pleadingly, said her name.

Her *old* name.

And what could she do after that? She rushed them.

The woman howled at the top of her lungs and barreled right towards the man with the knife. Shocked, he turned on her a moment too late. She slammed into him, knocking him over. The knife flew from his grasp. Michael picked it up and threw it at the nearest attacker. It caught him in the eye; he wailed as he went down.

Oh, God!

Two men left. Michael's heart seemed to explode with terror. He turned and fled while they tore the wom-

an he desperately needed to pieces.
    Doubly damned.

[CHAPTER 4]

BROKEN WOKE UP IN FULL DAYLIGHT, surrounded by her old body parts. Funny, her new arm looked thinner than the last. Maybe the old one had swelled up. The agony wasn't so intense this time; her body had already done most of its work.

The kid who had called her name sat next to her. He had a baby in a backpack plunked down next to him. He was dark-haired and short, and his face was thin, the features too close together. The baby had darker skin and deep black eyes, oddly intense.

"Silverwyng?" he said, voice shaking. "Um. You grew back. I'm glad."

She looked at him blankly.

"I've been looking for you," he continued. "Uh. You're going to help me and this baby get to Valen."

"Beh," said the baby.

Valen... that was... where? Wrong... something wrong...

"Broken," she whispered. "I'm not Silv... Broken..."

She blacked out again before he had a chance to respond.

◆►◄◆►

They huddled in a sleazy hash shop, clouds of pot smoke swirling all around them as the customers got wasted and ate tons of peanuts. Michael bought them both a joint, more for warmth than the relaxing high. The guy at the counter gave Michael a suspicious glare, but didn't ask for ID.

Broken took it as soon as he offered it to her, but otherwise didn't say a word. She glared at him and the baby suspiciously, as if they might suddenly explode or jump her or worse. Michael smoked hungrily, the effect blunting the edge of the depressing, desperate possibilities he saw all over the room.

At last he turned to her and said, without a trace of irritation, "Aren't you going to ask me *anything*?"

She just stared steadily at him, not blinking even once. Her eyes might dry out. Was she dead?

"I mean," Michael continued, feeling himself start to babble and not really caring, "I mean, don't you *wonder*? I came out of nowhere, with a baby, and I knew who you were. Oh, and those guys wanted to kill me. I got one with a knife." The thought made him mildly sick. He shoved it out of his mind.

Still Broken said nothing, sitting there like a statue of some ancient goddess of stubborn-ass dumpiness. He sighed and threw his arms up in the air. "Don't you want to know any of it? I know so much about you."

"I don't care," she said quietly. "You should go away."

The baby started to wail again. Other customers gave them dirty looks; Michael tried to soothe the child by picking him up and rocking him gently. Bad idea. Something foul dripped on his pants.

"Oh *hell*," he said. "Um. Look, I need to go clean him up. Wait here, okay? Please? Even if you don't, I'll still find you."

She looked away. He gave up and sprinted off to the bathroom.

Cleaning the kid made Michael throw up this time. When he finished, the shit and pee everywhere didn't seem quite as repulsive, but there it was nonetheless. Ugh. It wasn't until after he'd tossed the diaper in the wastebasket that he noticed the diaper pail, sighed, and dismissed it. Figured. He held the baby under the running water for a full minute, during which the kid managed to go again. Incredible. His mother must have fed him a steak before she killed herself.

Michael cleaned up as best as he could, and left the feces-covered bathroom with a slightly cleaner baby and an empty, queasy stomach.

Broken had gone. Surprise. He sighed again and stormed out into the cold after her.

She hadn't gotten far before collapsing. He found her face down in the middle of the crowded street. A light snow had started to fall.

"Sil—Broken?" he called softly, shaking her. "You there?"

She moaned and shook, and then was still again. She murmured something he couldn't make out.

"What?"

"H... hunnnn....rrrrr....."

Regenerating seemed to make her ravenous. "Hungry? You need food?"

She moaned weakly in response.

"Okay, just wait here, I'll see if I can get you something." He started to walk towards the hash shop, then turned and strode back to her.

"If I do this, you have to hear me out."

"Mmmrrr," she groaned. He took that as a yes.

"So whenever you regenerate yourself like that," he said as they slurped on greasy mystery sandwiches, "you get hungry. You need recharging, am I right?"

"Mmm," she said.

"Thought so. That must take an awful lot of energy. Does it hurt?"

"Fuhyoo," she said, mouth full.

"You too," he said mildly. "So, *now* do you want to know what's going on?"

She shook her head no. "M-mm."

"Not even a little bit? Really?"

"No!" she blared, sending bits of bread and meat

spattering onto Michael's face. He calmly wiped himself off. He'd had to deal with *much* worse today.

"Well, let me tell you anyway." She rolled her eyes and huffed, but kept eating. "My name is Michael Forward."

Broken snorted.

"I don't care what you think," Michael continued, miffed. "It is. Like you, I have abilities that most other people don't have. Unlike you, *mine* all still work."

She stopped chewing her food for a moment, then resumed.

"My power is," he paused for effect, "Seeing the future."

"Uh-huh," Broken intoned nasally.

"It's true," he said, glancing quickly at her and then away. Thousands of possibilities ricocheted through his mind. "I can see—I see all the ways things might turn out. I see futures that *could* happen for people. Don't you want to know what I see when I look at you?"

Broken gulped down her sandwich and stood up to go. "Bye," she said.

"You're important! You have to help me!" he called after her. "You have to help the baby!"

She paid no attention to him, but walked out the door and into the cold pre-dawn darkness.

He ran after her.

"If you help me—" he paused. "If you help me, I see you *flying* through the skies of Valen!"

She stopped dead.

"Broken—Silverwyng—please! I need your help. *We* need your help! If you help us, you *will* fly again. I've seen it."

Someone yelled something filthy down at him from a third-story window. Michael glanced up at him for a split second. The man was going to be hauled into jail tomorrow—all his futures said so.

When he looked back, all he could see of Broken was the swirl of her rags as she disappeared into an alley. He shouldered the baby and gave chase, but when he arrived he found nothing.

Michael, examining himself in the mirror, brushed a lock of dark brown hair back, and wished he had a comb. He looked terrible. There were dark circles under his eyes, and he seemed thinner and more worn than usual. A few pimples sprouted here and there on his cheeks and jaw. If he squinted, it kind of looked like the beginnings of a beard. He stroked his chin—still too smooth.

He tried to ignore the steady stream of possibility reflecting back at him. More than half of his futures lacked Broken, now.

He couldn't get the baby to Valen without her. Hell, they wouldn't last a week without her. The thin man would find them, take the baby and kill Michael. He had no idea what he could do to stop it.

For a moment, he considered going back to Union Tower and asking for Sky Ranger's help. But the Reformists had claimed the Union's leader, that much was obvious. No, Silverwyng—Broken—was the only help he could count on... unless something lay hidden in his flickering visions that he couldn't make out. He looked at the baby and strained to see more clearly. His head started to hurt, but nothing new came to him.

The baby started to cry again. He'd changed the boy twice in the last hour. How did the kid manage to crap himself so quickly? He'd also fed him some formula he'd picked up, but the kid spit it back up. Maybe he was hungry again. Michael sighed and made a silent vow to take the population-control fund's money and volunteer for a vasectomy if he ever got out of this.

He wrapped the last new diaper, around the baby and got out the bottle. It was ice cold. He'd heard somewhere that babies liked their formula warm, so he ran it under the hot water for a minute. It seemed to warm up slightly.

He glanced back in the mirror and started. Broken's face stared back at him.

"So," she grunted quietly, "Where are we going?"

He gathered himself quickly. "Uh. Delmarva, first."

She concentrated for a moment. "The spaceport. Long walk. You have money?"

"Not much," he admitted.

A weird grin cracked her face, then disappeared. "That ain't a problem."

He nodded, and risked a glance at his possibilities. Relief flooded through him. She was in all of them.

"So," she finally asked, "What's with the kid?"

[CHAPTER 5]

THEY WALKED SLOWLY, BROKEN awkwardly holding the softly gurgling baby against her filthy rags. Michael rattled off the places they needed to stop.

"Okay, first a store to buy diapers and baby food," he said. "Then some food for us. That might just about do it for my cash, though."

"You wanted to go to Delmarva with no cash?" she asked. "You can see the future; you should plan better."

True. But all the planning in the world couldn't make up for not actually having, much money to begin with. "I had some. I spent it getting here."

Broken looked amused. "Some fortune-teller."

"You shouldn't be holding him. You're filthy."

"Bite it," she said, but reluctantly handed him over. The baby mewled a bit, then seemed to fall asleep.

"What's his name?" Broken asked suddenly, with great interest.

Michael shrugged. "I have no idea. You want to give him one?"

"How'd you get a baby if you don't know his name?"

"His mother handed him off to me before squishing herself under a subway car," Michael explained.

"Oh," said Broken. "Why you?"

"Fate, I guess," Michael said with an air of nonchalance that he didn't really feel. "Also, I think there were some guys after her."

"Like the river," Broken said, more to herself than to Michael.

"Yeah, like them. Same sort of guys. They want the kid."

"Why?"

"They've got someone like me, I think. Maybe a little different, maybe someone who can see general possibilities. I just see possibilities for people I look at." He lowered his voice. "We're talking about the government, here. The Reformists, and their goons, the Black Bands. They want to make him into a monster."

"Okay," Broken said, unaffected by this devastating news.

"Don't you care that your own government wants to do this?" he asked, taken aback.

She shrugged. "Not really."

Michael shook his head, unable to make sense of her. "Go ahead and give the kid a name if you want. We'll never know what his mother called him."

Broken didn't say anything for a little while.

"Maybe... Ian?" she suggested shyly after some thought.

"Ian. All right, whatever."

"Or Joey. Matt. Buddy." She happily rattled off a list of names as they walked onwards. Michael sighed quietly. Ian it was.

There was a park in the middle of the Bronx, near the East River, where Broken claimed she'd hidden some money once. Michael was stuck carrying Ian while Broken led the way.

"Black Bands rally here," Broken hissed. "They come and go. It's their turf. We need to be quick." With the jerky quickness of someone who has been on the streets a long time, she darted over to a faded sign, and started fiddling around with the back.

Michael read the sign.

Yankee Park.
Site of New Yankee Stadium, home of the American League baseball New York Yankees, 2009-2040.
The Stadium was partially destroyed by bombs during the Last War 2046-7, and demolished 2056.
Park dedicated by the Metropolitan Recreation Authority, 2066.

Broken emerged from behind the sign with a brown paper bag and a smile. "Ready," she said. "What?"

Michael was shaking his head slowly back and forth. "I thought it was still standing."

"What?"

"Yankee Stadium."

Broken shrugged. "All the old stuff is destroyed around here. Manhattan used to be all skyscrapers, y'know, and Queens looked like this."

"How do you know?"

"Used to be a superhero," she said, turning her back on him and walking west.

"So we go down to Hampton Station and get on the rail, and head south to Wilmington. From there we can take ground trans to Delmarva Spaceport," Michael said, trying to keep up with her. "Okay?"

"Then?" Her cheery mood had disappeared as fast as it had come. Now she glowered and hid her face in her thicket of silver hair.

"Then we can get on a liner bound for Valen. Uh. One way or another."

"No plan," she said disgustedly.

"It's all we have," he said.

"Black Bands hang out at the station," she said. "Government runs the trains. If they want him, they can take him then."

Michael couldn't think of anything to say to that. She was right, of course. Another flash of devastating lucidity. Maybe she was less crazy than she seemed? Broken took one more step, glanced up—

—and pulled Michael into a doorway, flattening him as far into its recess as she could.

"What?"

"*Saw him,*" she said, a mixture of elation and fear in her voice.

Broken had been getting bored with this game. Michael Whatshisname didn't know what he was doing, and she didn't like babies much. Ian stank, and he cried all the time. She wanted to get away.

Then, out of the corner of her eye, she saw a hauntingly familiar shadow pass overhead.

Silverwyng and Sky Ranger flew high above the city.

"Did you know Manhattan used to be all skyscrapers?" he said. "Now it's just four-story apartments and condominiums. Queens was the low-rise part of town."

"Isn't that where the Tower is?"

"Yes. Queens is filled with tall buildings, now. It was where we rebuilt after the Last War." He was so confident, he sounded like he'd been there himself.

He chuckled quietly. "Progress is grand, isn't it? Nothing ever stays the same in this city."

Silverwyng actually found it a little depressing, but smiled at him anyway. Then, a horrifying jolt struck her.

For a split second, she lost power and plummeted towards earth. Sky Ranger stared, open-mouthed, as she dropped through the sky...

Sky Ranger, Michael thought desperately. It had to be.

"He's looking for us," she whispered. "He's looking for me."

"For you?" Michael snorted. "Not likely. He wants the baby."

"He has babies. He doesn't need mine." She snatched Ian out of Michael's arms and squeezed him so tight he cried out in confusion.

Michael sucked in his breath. They said Sky Ranger could hear even the smallest sounds from far away. Broken froze, eyes wide.

But the whoosh of air and the swirl of the hero's cape never came. When they dared to sneak out again, he had gone. Broken stared off to the east, where the distant spire of Union Tower peeked above the nearby buildings.

"That was stupid," Michael snarled. "He could have come. He could have taken him then."

"He's not one of them," Broken said. "He's no Black Band."

"Yes, he is!" Michael hissed. "How could you have missed that? He campaigned for Peltan last year, don't you remember?"

She shook her head stubbornly.

She fell, but did not scream. Sky Ranger receded. She reached a hand out to him. He could fly so fast, surely she would be saved.

He didn't move.

Suddenly, she felt whatever it was that kept her aloft return, and she powered back to where he was. Belatedly, he sped toward her. "Are you all right? You scared me."

"Oh," said Silverwyng. "I'm fine. Sorry."

He wouldn't look her in the eye. They both knew.

"He's good," Broken insisted. "I *knew* him."

Patrols combed the streets, endlessly searching—word of a double murder spread quickly. Police regulars and Black Bands guarded all the subway stations. A gauntlet lay between them and Hampton Station in Manhattan.

They'd spent most of the rest of the fleeting daylight hours running from one safe place to the next. At last, night fell and they could move more freely.

Broken was drunk. When they'd bought more baby food and diapers for Ian, she'd picked up ten tiny, plastic bottles of vodka, and had started downing them as soon as they'd managed to find a place to crash for the night.

This time it was one of the many abandoned buildings along the riverfront. They didn't dare turn on Michael's small flashlight, so the only light they had came from the silvery moon, far overhead, and the reflected glow of streetlights.

He heard her open another bottle. Was she crying? He checked on Ian; the baby slept peacefully. At least they had some money. It wasn't much, but it might get them to Delmarva Spaceport—if only they could get out of New York. How had she come by the money?

Better not to ask. He wasn't entirely sure she'd paid for all of those bottles of booze.

He read some of the graffiti on the walls, and tried to think about what to do next. He had Broken and the baby. That fulfilled part of the vision, and it was a huge achievement. But the rest...it seemed impossible. Broken wasn't fit for travel; he hadn't counted on that. When he'd tried to talk her out of drinking, she'd pretended he wasn't there. When he tried to take the bottles away, she almost bit his arm off. He rubbed the red marks absently.

So what now? How could he get to Delmarva with her?

He knew he couldn't get there without her. He glanced over at her.

—She knocked the pistol out of the man's hand.
—She watched over Ian and Michael while they slept.
—She let the Black Band beat her while Michael and Ian escaped.

Possibilities. She would make a difference. She had to; otherwise he would die before he ever saw Delmarva, and Ian would become a monster.

Too tired and worried to sleep, he distracted himself by looking around at the dilapidated old heap they were hiding in. The graffiti on the walls betrayed the building's age.

"God save us from China," read one.

"Fuck the bombs," read another.

"Nuke Beijing again!" read a third.

"Victory," prayed yet another. None of these things had come to pass; the people who had scrawled their desperate hopes on the walls had lost their war sixty years ago. He knew history. The million futures staring him in the face often drove him to the past, which was safely linear, and didn't fragment with each new development. What had happened stayed happened. Done was done.

As the possibilities approached the present, they became fewer and fewer, until, at the moment of passing, only one was left. Then it moved safely into the past, where he could remember and read about it, but never again see it unbidden whenever he looked at a face or glanced in the mirror.

He sighed. He hated the future.

From the first moment he'd looked in his mirror and seen not his reflection but the horrifying confluence of a million futures, this thread had enthralled him the most. He'd clung to it for all of his short life. Joe had done what he could to get Michael ready... and then the letter from Val Altrera had arrived, not long after Joe had died, and Michael had left his home to chase after a thin thread of hope in the form of a little orphan baby.

Hope against impossible hope.

Ian gurgled softly.

Broken sobbed in the corner. He thought about going to try and comfort her, but decided against it. He rubbed his aching arm again, and was glad he didn't have a mirror now. What he was likely to see would probably depress him terribly.

He glanced at Broken again. She'd fallen asleep. It figured.

—*The thin man stood opposite her.*
—*The thin man laughed, Ian in his arms.*
—*The thin man shot Michael.*
—*The thin man took Ian.*
—*The thin man shot Michael again.*
—*The thin man wrested Ian out of her grasp.*
—*The thin man shot her.*
—*The thin man took Ian from Michael's corpse.*

Every vision—! The thin man...

No. No... Michael tried to tear the vision from his mind. The thin man was death inescapable. He was in every single one of Broken's possibilities.

[CHAPTER 6]

MICHAEL BARELY SLEPT THAT NIGHT, waiting for the Black Bands or the police to come; they never did. Broken slept like the dead, and woke up in a far more lucid state.

"We should go," she said. She seemed remarkably refreshed, given the vast quantities of alcohol she'd consumed the previous night.

"Shouldn't you have a hangover or something?" he asked, cold and miserable.

"I don't get them," she said. "I heal."

Oh. Right. He shook his head and hated her a little. "Okay. Let's go."

"Where?" she asked.

He sighed, having been praying that she wouldn't ask him that question. "I don't know," he admitted. "I could hear patrols all night. I don't see how we could even get into the station, much less catch the rail to Delmarva. We may have to walk out of the city to another station somewhere."

They sat for a moment, thinking glumly about the prospect of hiking out of the city in winter.

"How's Ian?"

Ian hadn't moved much. Now he let out a soft whimper, and started crying pitifully.

Michael touched his forehead. "He's burning up! A fever."

A bad fever, too: Half his possibilities had gone dark. More were disappearing into yawning nothingness with each passing moment.

No! He has to live.

"Oh," said Broken.

"We could give him some medicine," Michael said, thinking out loud. But he didn't have anything, and the government monitored all the drugstores. They asked for ID, even for non-prescription meds.

"He ought to see a doctor," said Broken.

"You have any ideas? You need an ID to see doctors, too, and the cops can check that! I've used up the last of my fakes." Michael wanted to cry. All this... for nothing? Would Ian die before they ever got to Delmarva?

Would Michael be just a blip...?

Broken paced around the room for a minute. She looked terribly torn. Michael tried not to look at her.

"I know someone," said Broken at last. "I think she's still there." She set off purposefully towards the door in a swirl of silver hair and rags. Michael scooped up Ian and ran after her.

◆►◄◆

They made it to Yonkers after five torturous hours of slipping from building to building, keeping to the shadows and avoiding patrols. The broadcast screens mounted on the sides of buildings every block or so kept saying that the search was centered on Hampton Station. Maybe they'd confused whoever was after them.

The weather had turned even colder. Ian had stopped crying and hung limp in Michael's arms. So many possibilities... gone dark... the moment was coming soon.

He had started to think Broken was leading them around in circles when she turned down a nondescript side street, and banged on the door of a massive one-story house.

"Hey!" she called. "Hey!"

An older woman with short-cropped red hair opened the door.

"Yes?" She seemed very tired. "What do you want?"

"Hey there, Doctor Lucky Jane," said Broken. "Can you help us?"

The woman's eyes went wide. "S—Silverwyng?"

Broken smiled wide. "Hi. Got a sick baby. Can you help?"

The woman hesitated, and looked fretfully up and down the street before saying, "Um. Sure. Come in."

They were led into what looked like a living room. Couches and chairs were grouped together. Michael and Ian collapsed onto one of the softer couches. It felt so good to be warm again.

"Sil, what *happened* to you? I haven't seen you in... what, ten years? How did you find me? You look terrible." The red-haired woman sniffed. "And you need a bath."

"The baby," Broken reminded her.

"Is he yours?" She eyed the two of them suspiciously.

"Long story," grunted Broken. "Medicine first."

"Right. Is he sick? Let me see." She took the baby in her arms. "Oh! He has a serious fever. We should take him to the hospital."

Broken grabbed her arm. "No. No hospital. You. Here."

The slight woman hesitated, visibly warring with herself.

"Please, Lucky Jane," said Broken in perfectly even, lucid tones. Michael stared at her in shock; it was like a different person had spoken, her voice sweet and persuasive. "We need you. We can't go to anyone else."

The woman—Jane?—closed her eyes and dipped her head. "I see. Okay. Fine. Let me find something here that will bring the fever down." She disappeared into another room.

"You know her?" Michael asked.

"Yuh," Broken assented. "Lucky Jane. She was a doctor back at the Tower." She'd found a bowl of fruit and was cramming an apple into her mouth.

"She's from the Union?" Michael started to panic. He had thought the Union people were all in the Tower. That was the law, wasn't it? Why was there one here? Was she going to go call Sky Ranger?

Broken nodded again, but didn't elaborate. The

woman came back.

"Here. Let's try this." She put a green slow-release patch on Ian's arm. "That should bring the fever down. Look. He really should go see a doctor."

"*You're* a doctor," Broken said.

"Well, uh, I, ah, I'm *sort* of a doctor," Lucky Jane stammered. "Not much of one, really. I don't practice anymore. Not since..."

"Still a doctor," Broken said. "Always. You can't not be one."

The woman shrugged and sat, cradling the baby in her lap. She wrinkled her nose.

"I'll get that," Michael volunteered. "Got a bathroom?"

"It's... it's all right," she said, a faraway look in her eyes. I should examine him a little more closely anyway. Be right back. Lydia is here, too, she might come in." She carried Ian out of the room. He started crying again, which was a good sign. They heard the woman make happy, disgusted noises from the bathroom.

"Are you *sure* this is safe?" Michael hissed.

Broken glanced over. "Safe," she assured him.

Possibilities came and went, none of them useful. He sighed. He'd have to trust her for now.

"Nice house," Michael said, to fill the silence.

"Belongs to her *rhi*," said Broken.

"Her what?"

"*Rhi*," Broken said, irritated. "Räton marriage. I used to watch this place, knew *she* was here. There's maybe seven of them."

"Oh. Räton marriage?" Michael had never met a Räton. He knew that the Reformists hated them, though.

What had he heard about Räton marriages?

Seven people? Were they all married to one another? That sounded familiar. The Reformists had been making a big deal out of that sort of thing. *Alien.*

He picked up a small pamphlet on the coffee table.

"The Räton Family—An Alternative for Humans" read the title.

This place had its own literature? He skimmed through it.

The Räton family is MISUNDERSTOOD and much maligned, even by those in our own government. The following an except from Andrew Angstrom's FAMOUS study of the rhi:

Räton Family Structure and Politics
From the Journal of Xenocultural Studies v.12(2) (©2091 Sydney Univ. Press)

Ever since the landing of the *Mathapavanka* in 2050, humans have been flummoxed by Räton family structure and internal politics. This guide should help the curious human to understand more about the complex relationships that underlie Räton society.

1. Family units

The basic Räton family unit is not, as it is for most humans, the nuclear assemblage of two married parents and their children. Nor is it an extended family of grandparents, cousins, aunts and uncles. Räton families are called rhi, which means "circle". The rhi often contains a dozen or more individuals who are bound together in a socioeconomic, sexual, and legal relationship (something like human and Rogarian marriage), along with the children who ultimately result from their couplings.

Despite claims by certain religious and moral groups, the Räton *rhi* is nothing like historical human polygamy. One male does not marry several wives. Indeed, most rhi contain an equal number of men and women, all of whom are permitted and encouraged to have sexual relations with one another. There is sometimes a hierarchy in the rhi, but where it appears, it is usually based on ability and seniority rather than gender. The entire rhi raises the children, who rarely know exactly who their biological parents are. It seems to be enough to know that they are genetically part of the rhi. When questioned on the subject, most Rätons were either uninterested in or somewhat skittish about the "act of biology" that had brought them into this life.

Additionally, the members of the rhi all will usually share the same vocation or related group of vocations. For example—

Ugh. How boringly alien. He put the pamphlet down. No wonder everyone hated the Rätons.

And yet here they were in a house occupied by a Räton-style *rhi,* while the Reformists and their goons were looking for Ian. Great.

Broken seemed right at home. She had stretched out on a couch, where she had promptly fallen asleep. The beige couch was turning a nice shade of dull gray from the crud caked on her clothes.

Lucky Jane re-entered the room. "Oh! Sil, honey, could you—uh, could you not...?"

"She can't help it," Michael said. "She's been living on the streets."

"Oh! I, uh... Really?"

"Why don't you give her a shower and wash her clothes?" Michael suggested evenly. "She was your friend, right?"

"Well... yes... but that was a long time ago."

"No friend like an old friend. She won't steal anything. How is Ian?"

"Ian? Oh, the baby? Uh. Do you have any food?"

Michael rummaged around in his pack, which still smelled faintly of Ian excreta. Had it really been two days since he'd last been clean and warm? "Yeah. Here." He tossed a can of cheap baby formula her way. She fumbled it, and it rolled away under one of the couches; she had to kneel to find it.

Another woman entered. She was plump and middle-aged, and wore the expression a nun might have upon finding semen splattered on the communion wafers. "*Jane!*" she gasped. "What is going *on?* Who are these people?"

"Uh," the red-haired woman stuttered, bumping herself on the couch as she hurriedly straightened, "Uh, they're—er—they're some friends, Lydia. Old friends."

"They look like bums," Lydia whispered, too loudly.

"*She's* a bum," Michael said, pointing a foot at the sleeping Broken. "I'm just... I'm passing through."

Jane took Lydia by the shoulder and hissed a few things in her ear. Michael thought he heard the word "baby" a few times. Lydia's expression didn't change.

"Why not the hospital?" Lydia demanded. "Why here?"

Michael made the mistake of looking at her, and their eyes met.

—*Fire.*
Fire.
"FIRE. FIRE! FIRE!!"
"Burn them! Alien-loving garbage!"
Her skin blackened and crisped as she lost the ability to scream anymore. She lived for another two full minutes of purest agony before death mercifully carried her away.

He reeled, gasping. "Ah!"

"Well?" Lydia advanced on him. He noticed that she had a small, light blue pin on her jacket. "UNP," it read. "Why not the hospital? Are you criminals?"

"No," he whispered, stunned and trying to shake the image he'd just experienced. "No."

"Then *why?*"

Michael gambled. "The Black Bands are looking for us. Political trouble."

Lydia's face darkened. "I see!" she said, regarding him a little more kindly. "The Reformists have no respect for anyone. What did you do?"

"I—" What would sound good to this kind of woman? "I painted a picture of Peltan," he said. "With *blood* on his mustache. The Black Bands wanted to burn it, so I—I *punched* one of them and ran. They're after both of us."

"Good for you!" Lydia said viciously. "No wonder you look so terrible. An artist! So few artists these days. Well. You can stay here until the 'heat is off,' as they say, and your—your?— baby gets better. I'll talk to Andrew."

"Thank you, Lydia," Jane said softly. She returned to the bathroom, where Ian was starting to howl again.

"Broken," Michael said. "Wake up."

She stirred briefly. "Wha...?"

"We can't stay here long," he whispered. "This place won't last. They're going to be killed by a mob. I don't know when. Soon, maybe."

"Oh. Okay." Broken dropped back to sleep. He doubted she'd registered a thing he'd said.

What was it Joe called me? Cassandra? How appropriate.

[CHAPTER 7]

THE REST OF THE RHI ARRIVED AS night crowded out the short, cold day.

Andrew, the patriarch, came home first. Michael knew guys like Andrew. He was maybe fifty, maybe sixty. It was hard to tell. He wore very neat clothes in a deliberately casual fashion. His gray hair was close-cropped, and he wore spectacles perched low on his nose. Since most men of Andrew's class could afford corrective surgery, the glasses were likely an affectation.

He glanced at Michael and the sleeping, but now cleaner, Broken, who was wearing one of Jane's pink sweatsuits; Jane had managed to wake her up just long enough to get her to shower and change. A solitary "Oh!" escaped his lips before Lydia dragged him over to the corner, where they conversed animatedly for about a minute. Lydia's part of it was animated, anyway. Andrew mostly just stood there and nodded, every once in a while raising a finger to interject a word or two. When they returned, he greeted Michael warmly.

"An artist, is that so?" he asked. Michael nodded warily. This "artist" thing was going to lead to trouble, he knew it. What if they wanted him to paint a picture? He could always fake artist's block. Did artists get blocked? Maybe a wrist injury.

"We have a few spare rooms in the house," he said, a little too jovially. "You can each have one. That's the Räton way; everyone needs to have their own *zha*. yes? Have you read the pamphlet we put out?" He indicated the booklet on the table that Michael had glanced at.

"Some of it," Michael said.

"Well, then, you know what we're all about! I wrote most of the articles it cites, you know. I used to be a lecturer on the subject at Sydney University; I've been to Räta, and lived amongst the Rätons themselves. Such an experience! Of course, with things the way they are, it's unlikely I'll get back any time soon. You say you painted Peltan with blood? How rich! Well, it may be true soon enough. But let's get you something to eat. Lyddie, have they eaten?"

"No," Lydia said. "They can have dinner with the rest of us in an hour. I'm not making another meal; we can't afford it."

"Lyddie over here keeps the books," Andrew said to Michael. "She's a slave-driver, I tell you!"

Michael grinned weakly.

"So where's that baby?" Andrew asked, looking around. "Been a while since we had a baby here!"

"With Jane," Lydia said. "She's keeping an eye on

him."

"That's good. Is he yours?" Andrew said, casting a suddenly critical eye on Michael.

"No. Nor hers," Michael said, indicating Broken. "Orphan."

"Oh? And what are you doing with him?"

Michael cursed himself for not thinking of an answer to that question sooner. He hadn't planned any of this very well, had he? He had a tendency to assume the future would take care of itself. In his visions, it always did, somehow. Planning seemed irrelevant; no matter how many plans people made, they always fell victim to forces beyond their control. That was life. That was fate.

Still, he of all people should know better. How many deaths came from carelessness?

Michael gambled on a version of the truth. "His mother gave him to me. Right before she died. I promised to care for him."

Andrew nodded thoughtfully. "A big task for someone so young. How old *are* you?"

"Eighteen," Michael lied.

"A big task indeed. Look, let me show you to your rooms. Er. What's your friend's name?"

"She calls herself 'Broken,' " said Michael. "I don't know her real name."

"Oh. Well! I'll call her 'B,' perhaps. Come on, B, wake up. Let me show you a room where you can sleep more comfortably."

Broken stirred and stood. It was a miracle. She followed after them, still mostly asleep.

◆▷▶ ◀◁◆

The house, which Andrew sometimes called the "*rhizhandl,*" was arranged as a square of rooms built around a glassed-in inner courtyard. A hallway ran around the edge of the courtyard. The private rooms of each member of the *rhi* and the common areas, like the kitchen and the living room, were on the other side of the hallway from the courtyard, on the outer side of the house. Andrew explained that each *rhin* got his or her own room, and that very few of them ever slept together at night, because of the Räton concept of *zha,* or personal space. He launched into an impromptu lecture on *zha* and its relation to the *rhi* and house construction, which delayed them from reaching their first destination for at least five minutes.

"Here we are," he said at last. This hallway was opposite the courtyard from the communal rooms, and had four rooms in it. Andrew opened one of the doors. "I can't give you a key," he explained. "Just for safety. Your safety. Of course! So. Who wants this one?"

Broken barged in and collapsed on the bed. She was asleep before she hit the pillow.

"This one's hers," Michael said, unnecessarily.

"Ah, um, yes. I see! Good night, B! We'll call you for dinner." He closed the door quietly. "Let me show you to your room, Mike. Is Mike all right, can I call you Mike?"

Michael shrugged. "Sure." He hated the nickname, but figured he ought to put up with it out of politeness. He was an uninvited guest, after all, and a fugitive, no less.

"I had this house built in 2096, when I came back from Sydney," he said, gesturing at various bits of odd statuary and architectural flourishes. "I loved the Räton style so much, I had to build an homage to it. Doesn't it make more sense than our own fractured way of living? Four to a house, maybe five? And that includes children! Ha! So lonely." He sighed. "We had children here before the government took them away. I miss them so. Having your little Ian here will be wonderful for us, even for a only few days."

He turned the corner and led Michael into a newer wing of the house. "When we had children, we had to expand the house," he explained. "They're all gone... but we're keeping their rooms just the way they were, just in case. You never know! Right?"

"Right," Michael said.

"Right," repeated Andrew emphatically. "Here. It's a bit lonely back here, but Monica will be next door to you. Knock on the wall if you need anything. All right? I'll let you get settled."

"Hey," said Michael. "Where will Ian be?"

"Jane will take care of him. She's really good with babies. If that's okay, of course." A shadow passed across his jovial features. "It would be very good for her to have him for a while. Something she needs. Unless you wanted him back right away?"

"No, that's fine," Michael assured him. A vacation from baby poop! That he could live with.

"All right. Dinner in an hour. You'll be able to smell it." Andrew left Michael alone in the small, rectangular room. He hadn't really been alone in days.

There was a bed next to a large window, which overlooked a neglected garden and an empty pool. Some children's toys were scattered here and there in the courtyard. What was it Andrew said? The government had apparently taken the children who had lived here away. Michael wondered why. Had the adults done something, committed some crime...? Or was it because of the unusual living arrangements? Could be either.

There was no mirror in the room. He thanked whatever gods tormented him that they'd spared him that, at least. His own room, back home, had featured a full-length mirror attached to the wall opposite his bed. He covered it up whenever he could, but the covering never stayed up for long. He often woke up and instantly saw ten different versions of his own demise. Getting ready for school after that usually seemed moot.

He heard voices in the hallway nearby. One was Andrew. The other he didn't recognize. The voices stopped. The door of the room next to his shut, and fast-paced Räton-inspired pop music bled through the walls. This wasn't the scary hardcore music the Black Bands and their buddies listened to—this was softer, more lilting and much more peaceful. Virtually nobody admitted listening to it anymore.

That had to be Monica. Michael wondered what the rest of this *rhi* would be like. What kind of people defied society and lived like Rätons these days? Strange ones, he decided. Or ones with a death wish.

—*Fire.*
—*Fire. Fire.*

He shuddered, picturing the room in flames. How long? How much time...? Could they be saved? Would it even happen?

The music from next door stopped. A knock on

his door followed. A girl, not too much older than him, stood in the hallway. She had dyed black hair, freckles, green eyes, and a sort of lopsided smile. She wore nothing but shades of purple.

"I'm Monica," she said. "Nice to meet you. Andrew said you were staying with us."

"Yeah," he said, smiling. "Nice, uh, to meet you." He tried to push *fire* out of his mind. Control, control!

"Can I come in?"

"Um, sure." He let her pass into "his" room.

"Oh, how weird!" she exclaimed. "This room was so different when John lived here. He had all these shelves over there, they were so neat."

"Who was John?" asked Michael.

Monica's expression turned sour. "One of us. A *rhin*. He left last year, after the election. He said he couldn't stay in the Confederation anymore, so he went to Räta. We haven't heard from him in a while, but he got there safe. I still kind of miss him. He was nuts, but he had a good sense of humor."

He may have been wise, Michael thought. Once a man who vowed that anyone who followed Räton culture was a traitor was elected president of the Confederation... well, life could get complicated. He wondered why the rest hadn't gone with him.

Monica sat on the bed. "Lyddie is cooking tonight. Have you met her?" Michael nodded. "She can be demanding, but she's okay, really. Don't let her get to you. Hey, I'm glad you're letting Jane take care of the baby. That's going to be really good for her."

"Andrew said that, too," Michael said. "How come? What happened?"

Deep sadness shadowed Monica's cherubic face. "Our kids. Jane bore all three of them. Lyddie isn't fertile, and Janeane and I don't want to get pregnant. Jane's been really depressed ever since they were taken."

"Ah," said Michael. That made sense. Time to change the subject. "So. Uh. How long have you been here?"

"Only eighteen months or so. I'm the youngest. It's a nice setup, don't you think? We used to have so many more people. All the rooms were full when I joined. It's kind of sad, but at least there's lots of room now. I was the only one left in the back hallway since they took Violet and John left. Fred used to say he'd move back here with me... but he never did. Too lazy. You'll meet Fred tomorrow morning; he works a late shift."

"Why'd you decide to join a, uh, *rhi*, if you don't mind my asking?"

Monica smiled crookedly again. "Andrew was a professor of mine at City College. After he got laid off, I felt bad for him, so I came out here to visit. I fell in love with it. I'd always loved his lectures about Räton culture... Anyway, they let me stay a few days, then offered me a place in the family a little later."

Creepy, Michael thought, against his will. He quashed the image.

Monica continued: "I've always been glad they took me in... even now, when things aren't so good." She flopped over and lay on the bed. "Andrew's been so sad lately. Maybe having new people around will cheer him up."

"Maybe," Michael said. Monica was acting like they were planning to stay. He didn't dissuade her.

"So how did *you* come here? Kind of a strange place to end up."

"Broken knew Jane from before, I guess."

Monica sat up, interested. "No way! Really? No one knows *anything* about Jane, especially what she used to do. Is 'Broken' the one Andrew calls 'B'?"

"Yes. I'm not sure why."

"Oh, he likes to give people nicknames. You'll see. So, got any stories about Jane from before? What did she do? What was she like?"

Michael shrugged. "No idea. I didn't know her; Broken did. She doesn't talk much about the past, either."

"Is she really a bum? Lyddie said she was."

"She is," Michael confirmed. "But she wasn't, once."

◆►◄◆

Dinner came, and the entire *rhi*, plus Michael, crowded into the kitchen to eat. "Rätons don't have a separate room for dining," explained Andrew, though Michael hadn't asked. "That's why the house doesn't have one. In fact, they often eat alone. But we like to be together at dinner, so we are."

"Ah," said Michael. The food looked edible, at any rate. Whatever it was Lydia was slathering onto their plates, it sure had lots of sauce.

"Is your, ah, friend joining us?" Andrew asked.

"Couldn't wake her. She'll be out for leftovers," Michael said, helping himself to a roll.

"Well, then. Everyone, this is Mike. He and his friend B are going to be joining us for awhile. They have a baby that Jane is taking care of." He beamed proudly. "Mike is a political dissident. An anti-Reformist *artist*."

There were grunts of assent all around the table.

"Mike, you've met Lyddie, Jane, and my *Lyasti*—that's Monica." Each one of them nodded in turn.

"My nickname means 'little student,'" Monica explained to him.

—Fire...

"Let me introduce Shawn, who's on your left." Shawn nodded. He was of medium height, with sandy brown hair and a surly expression. He was probably in his thirties, Michael guessed.

—Fire...!

"Over here is Janeane."

"Hello." Janeane said. She was a tiny, dark-skinned woman with a smooth, shaved head and bright, expressive eyes. Michael couldn't look away from them.

—Waves lapped against the shore. The sea rose and fell in the distance. The tide came in and went out. The world turned, and everything was quiet, calm, peaceful...
—Endless sea.
—Peace...

What? Michael blinked, clearing his vision.

The corners of Janeane's mouth quirked up as she studied him through half-lidded eyes. He resolved to look into her a little more closely.

"Fred isn't here. He works a night shift; he's a security guard down at the electronics outlet. But he's a
nice guy, he'll stop in and say hi before he goes to bed."
Andrew beamed again. "Let me just say how wonderful
it is to have new people in the house, our *rhizhandi*. It is
especially joyous for me to have a baby here, even if it is
only temporary."

"Agreed," murmured Janeane. Her voice was soft,
rich and low. Michael immediately hoped she'd speak
again.

"Hear, hear," Monica added, glancing at Jane. Ian
was bouncing and gurgling on her lap. Jane smiled down
at him and made little nonsense noises. Michael noticed
that she hadn't eaten a bite during the meal.

He felt an overwhelming urge to leap up on the
table and beg them to leave the house any way they
could, as fast as they could. He wanted desperately to
tell them about *fire* and the approaching mob. But why
would they believe him? Only Broken seemed to believe
him when he talked about his visions. *Cassandra.*

Shawn didn't say anything to Michael throughout
the meal, which was just as well. Michael got the impression that Shawn didn't like him much. Janeane chat-
ted idly with everyone as they ate, and asked Michael a
string of questions about where he was from, what he
had done to be on the run, how he got started as an artist, and on and on. Michael made up a number of stories
he hoped he could remember later. He tried to keep it as
simple as possible.

He could hear Joe's voice: *Complicated lies never
hold up.* Joe had always been full of practical advice.

Lydia seemed more interested in Andrew's day than in Michael, Broken, or Ian. It turned out that Andrew worked in a store in Queens, selling jewelry. So much for the professor. His day hadn't gone well, and Lydia spent some time comforting him. Meanwhile, Monica and Janeane talked about Janeane's job at the Colonization Authority, which had a processing station in Newark. She was, from what little Michael could tell, a bureaucrat of some minor importance. Monica was apparently unemployed, as were Lydia and Jane. He had no idea what Shawn did.

During the meal, Michael did his best to keep the distressing images of *fire* out of his mind. He focused on Janeane, just because her possibilities were so impossibly *calm*.

He had never met anyone who had nothing of sorrow in their future. Just an endless ocean... bobbing peacefully... then nothing. All her paths led there—in fact, they started there, too. It was as if she had no paths at all...or Michael simply couldn't read her. But that was impossible. He had never met anyone who was unreadable.

When dinner ended, he retreated to his room, remembering to thank Lydia for the meal before he went. He lay down on his bed and found himself dozing off.

—*Fire...*

—*The house burned around them. He could hear Andrew shouting, panicked, as he searched for Lydia. Shawn banged on a door, only to find it barred shut from outside. The mob chanted, only barely audible over the roar of the flames. Monica sat on the floor*

with Jane in her arms as they waited for death.
"My fault!" Jane wailed.
—*Janeane floated on the ocean, far, far away...*
—*Far away...*
—*Bob up and down, the water cool and refreshing...*
—*A brilliant blue sky... no clouds, no worries... far*
away... her family was dying. But Janeane was safe.
Janeane would always be safe. She carried them in
her heart, though she couldn't carry them with her.
She carried them safe to shore.

A knock on the door. Michael sprang awake. The
house still stood.

"Michael?" It was Janeane. Of course. He opened
the door and let her in. "Well. I like what you've done
with the place," she said.

"I haven't done anything," Michael protested.

"That's what I like. Mind if I sit?"

"Go ahead."

She pulled the chair away from the beat-up desk,
and sat down in it. The beauty and peace of her possibilities overwhelmed Michael. Janeane smiled lightly,
her soft features blending into the endless sea of her
future...

"You were staring at me during dinner," she said,
her voice like shimmering, sun-soaked water. "Kind of
like you're staring at me now."

"Oh? Uh." Michael shook his head. "Sorry. It isn't
what you think." Or was it? She was beautiful. He hadn't
ever met a woman he found *really* beautiful, not in this
way.

"It isn't? That's too bad. Although you're a little

young. How old are you?"

"F-fourteen," he stammered, forgetting to lie.

"Thought so. Andrew said you were older." Her grin sparkled against her dark cheek. "So what's your story?"

"I..." he began. "I... uh... I'm an artist..."

She laughed. It was the most remarkable sound he'd ever heard, the sound of crashing waves and delicate windchimes in the ocean breeze. "Sure you are. Tell me true. Where are you, a bum, and a baby who doesn't belong to either of you going? Why are you on the run from the bully boys?"

He leveled his gaze at her. "Janeane... tell me about the sea."

"You first," she admonished him lightly.

Flustered, he looked at the floor. "You won't believe it. But..."

"Yes?" She waited expectantly, like a goddess perched on the throne of eternity.

"I see people's futures. Things that could possibly happen to them."

She arched an eyebrow. "A fortune teller?"

"No!" he laughed. "Well, not really. What I see is real."

Janeane shrugged. "My aunt Clara was a fortune teller. She saw all kinds of stuff. Some of it came true, some of it almost came true. You know? Are you like her? *Special?*" The word dripped with meaning.

Michael nodded. He was sweating. Time seemed to be slowing to a crawl all around him. He thought of lies and evasions, but none of them made it to his lips. "Yes. Like that."

"So what did you see, fortune teller? Or would you rather I call you 'prophet?'"

He reddened. "I... uh. Ian. The baby. I saw something about him."

"Where'd he come from?"

"A woman—his mother—she gave him to me. In a subway station. She just handed him to me." He took a deep breath. "I'd been... waiting for him. He's also, um. Special. But in a different way."

"What happened to his mom?" Janeane asked.

"Train got her." Janeane arched that eyebrow again, but said nothing. "He... he could be either a great man of peace, bringing everyone together... leading billions to freedom. Or... he could be a terrible monster."

"And you want to make him into a saint." Janeane said softly. The sea swirled all around her.

"No," Michael said. "I'm taking him off-planet, to Valen. Someone else will do the rest. I just have to get him there."

He was telling her everything. She could tell anyone; she could turn him in, destroy him. But somehow he wasn't afraid.

"What's on Valen?"

"Someone who will make him into a saint," Michael said. "I don't know any more than that."

"And Jane's friend?"

"I need her. She... she was in every vision of success. I don't know why... not really."

They regarded one another for a long moment.

"So, the sea," Janeane said smoothly, voice like a rushing wave. "The sea...I've always seen the ocean. I love the ocean."

"That's all I see for you. Everyone else has death, fear, hope, despair... horrible things. Wonderful things. It's... so strong, sometimes. But you!" Michael desperately wanted to take one of her slender hands in his. "You are so calm. Nothing but the ocean. Peace. It's beautiful."

She smiled knowingly.

"I could look at you all day! You're so beautiful!" Michael said, feeling a dam threaten to break inside him. "It— I—"

He regained his control. "Sorry."

She planted a cool kiss on his forehead. He almost fainted, but looked up into her deep brown eyes instead. Miles and miles of calm, placid sea reflected back at him. She placed a single finger on his heart. "When you need me, I'll be here."

She let herself out of the room. Michael shuddered. He was drenched in his own sweat.

The tide ebbed; the ocean receded. He felt cold and alone.

Doubt started to creep in. Who would she tell? Who was listening? Joe had always told him to play his cards close to his chest. Don't reveal what you don't absolutely have to, never ever tell someone the truth of what you are and what you can do. Now he'd all but given his entire hand to a woman he'd only just met.

He collapsed on his bed. There was nothing for it, now. He rummaged in his pack and held the mirror up to his face.

—Terror, death, fire, victory.

Janeane would not betray him. Not that he could see. He breathed a sigh of relief, and went to find Broken.

[CHAPTER 8]

BROKEN OPENED THE DOOR AT THE knock. Her silver hair was disheveled, and she tasted nothing but beer in her mouth. It was kind of the previous occupant of the room to hide alcohol everywhere.

"Can I come in?" he asked. She shrugged and stood aside.

"How are you?" Michael asked.

Again she shrugged.

"Did you sleep well?" Shrug. "Did anyone come to see you?"

"Andrew did. Three times."

Michael nodded, seeming to think that was significant. "How about Jane?"

Broken felt a little pang. "Nope."

"She's probably busy with Ian. So you knew her before?"

Broken nodded, struggling to keep herself lucid. "She was Doc's assistant. We called her 'Lucky.' Because she was."

"That was her, um, ability?"

"Good for a doctor."

"So why isn't she there anymore?"

Broken shrugged again. "Luck went bad."

Michael digested that. "You mean, she used to have really good luck and now she has really bad luck?" Broken nodded. "Wow. That's awful."

Worse, Jane was like a walking curse now. But Broken thought better of mentioning that.

"Maybe... maybe we ought to get out of here soon," Michael suggested.

"Safe for now," Broken said. "I want to sleep. Jane gave me some clothes."

"That's good. But we shouldn't stay here too long, okay?"

Broken nodded and turned her back to him. She wanted to be alone. He got the message and left.

Broken lay on the bed and thought about Jane.

"Hey, Doctor Lucky Jane!" Silverwyng waved jauntily to Lucky, who was filling out some forms at her desk.

"Hey, Sil," Lucky replied. "Back so soon?"

"Yeah." Silverwyng plopped down in Lucky's spare chair. "Boring patrol, no one out there."

Lucky lowered her voice. "Did it happen again?"

A shadow passed over Silverwyng's normally happy features. "No. Not this time. Hey, did... did Sky Ranger say *anything? About me? He was in here earlier."*

"How do you know that?"

Silverwyng grinned sheepishly. "Stole a look at your schedule."

Lucky sighed. "You should stay out of there. Doc will kill you, and me." She reached out a cupped hand next to the table, just as Silverwyng knocked a pencil holder off it. Lucky caught it deftly in her waiting palm. "No. He didn't say anything. Should he have? What's going on with you two?"

Silverwyng looked like she was about to cry. "Nothing," she managed before flying out of the room.

"Hey, Sil," said a familiar voice at the door.

Broken's face cracked into a grin. "Hey, Doctor Lucky Jane."

"So." Jane came and sat on Broken's bed. "What are you calling yourself now, 'Broken?' What's happened to you these past ten years?"

"Long story," Broken said. "You know how it started."

"Yeah. You couldn't fly. I remember." Jane sighed. "I'm sorry, Sil. We tried so hard to fix it."

"I know."

"I left not long after. My luck... it went away. It turned on me, bad enough that I became a danger. Bad enough that they didn't chase me when I left, even with the rules. So I know how you feel."

"Yeah." Broken and Unlucky stared at one another for a long, long moment.

"How's Ian?" Broken asked.

"Better," Jane said.

"Good."

"This is terrible," Jane said. "I've really missed you. Why didn't you come see me before? You obviously knew where I was."

Broken shook her head. "Sorry."

"Have you really been living on the streets?"

"Yeah."

"Sil, that's no way to live. You should have come here. We'd have taken you in."

Broken shrugged.

Jane stood, suddenly angry. "You could have come here! I didn't fall apart completely after my powers went! Even though everything I touch goes bad, I still kept *living!* You can't fly, so you're *normal*, but you go to pieces! I don't understand you, Sil. Why didn't you come to me?"

"I couldn't," was all Broken could say, long after Jane had stormed out of the room. "I'm sorry."

Silverwyng and Sky Ranger sliced through the air.

"What makes us special," Sky Ranger said, "Is this."

"It would be awful to be just normal," agreed Silverwyng.

That night, as he tried to sleep, fire scorched through Michael's dreams. He tried to escape, but found no way out. All the exits were blocked.

And then, his dream burbled and gulped, and he

was on a quiet seashore. Birds called overhead, the waves rushed at the sand, the sun shone lazily on his upward-tilted face.

Janeane sat on the bed next to him, slid in beside him. Peace enveloped Michael as her lips pressed against his. The sea roared, the waves crashed.

He could not remember such utterly calm happiness, even as their bodies started to move together.

She stayed with him that night, and the next, and the next...

Michael pushed Ian and Delmarva out of his mind. He forgot about fire. Janeane filled him with calm and peace.

They stayed at the house longer than they'd planned. They stayed until cold 2106 bled into colder 2107. Being near Janeane, Michael had lost his sense of urgency. All he wanted to do was be near her. She was so peaceful. He had never known peace like hers.

Broken flitted around the house like a demented ghost for a week straight, then stopped. She still wasn't speaking with Jane. Whenever Jane came near, Broken hid.

From time to time, Michael stood near her door and listened to her weep quietly.

I want no part of other people's pain, Michael thought. *At least, not any more than I have already.* And he went to find Janeane, or to sit where she had been and absorb more of her peace.

The others seemed not to notice that they had stayed far beyond what they had originally said. Every morning, Andrew would come to Michael's room and smile, saying, "You're welcome to stay longer."

And Michael would say, "Thank you." And they'd stay longer. Michael had no wish to hurl himself back into the freezing world. He started to avoid Ian and Broken, and stopped looking in the mirror.

Whenever he saw *fire* licking at the edges of his vision, he ran for Janeane so he could see the ocean rocking back and forth, bobbing up and down, over and over...

Janeane was always happy to see him. Sometimes, as he lay tossing and turning from his dreams, she would put her cool hands on his forehead, and whisper things he didn't understand in his ears. "This is for you, Prophet," she said. "Only for you."

Sometimes she seemed tired and haggard, but whenever Michael or Monica asked her about it, she put them off, saying she'd just had a long day. She'd been having a lot of long days, lately.

Outside, the world was tilting sharply downwards. But Michael took no notice of it. He rarely ventured out into the cold. He tuned out the hushed, heated discussions of politics and Reformists. What did he care for them? He was safe here.

Broken came to him just after the new year. "Ian," she said. "Valen."

She looked cold, determined, insistent. He waved

her off.

"Soon," he promised. "Let me rest. We'll go soon."

"Men," she grumbled, and wandered off.

At times, he did venture outside with Monica. She liked to take walks down to a nearby pond, where she could feed the few ducks that remained.

"So tell me about Janeane," he said one cold January day. The pond hadn't frozen over completely, so the ducks were still bobbing on its surface. Michael and Monica tossed bread crumbs at them; they picked them out of the air when they could, and swam hard after them when they missed.

"Oh, she's a friend of mine from when I was in college," Monica said. "She's older than me, but we got along really well.. She kind of got me involved with the *rhi*. At least, that's how I got interested in one of Andrew's Xenoculture classes. Janeane kept bugging me to go. And so I did. I guess it's hard to not do what Janeane says." She laughed.

"Yeah," Michael agreed. The ocean roared in his memory.

"She's not from around here. I think she grew up somewhere a lot warmer, in the south or maybe the Caribbean. She never said, and I didn't ask. She likes to keep secrets."

"Mmm," Michael said. He could see that.

"How's your friend? B?"

"Fine... I think. I see her creeping around the house at night, and she's been getting drunk a lot, but she's not stealing anything and she's still around. I guess that's a start."

Monica giggled, her green eyes bright. "Jane won't talk about her anymore. All she does is play with Ian. It's like she has a new kitten."

"I'm glad Ian's happy," Michael said, tuning out. Ian... Ian...

—There was a man signing a piece of paper. There would be peace and unity for a century. Peace...

He let himself relax and forgot about it.

Broken knocked on his door one day not long after. She was completely sober; her gaze was hard and quick.

"Hey. We should go," was all she said.

Michael shook his head. "We need to make sure Ian is all better. Patience. I'm still coming up with a plan." He seemed out of it, his eyes faraway and dreamlike.

Broken grunted and left.

She passed Janeane in the hallway later that day, and glared at her. Janeane only smiled; she was infuriatingly difficult to hate.

That night she dreamed of lying on a beach, and then of wading in shallow water that came to her knees. Was there something there, in the water? She reached for it.

She woke abruptly, feeling a sense of incalculable, unknowable loss.

Something inside her began to shift.

◄►► ◄◄►

Janeane and Michael lay in bed, listening to the quiet of the house around them. He ran his hands along the soft curve of her side, and she moved closer to him in her sleep, murmuring happily.

"I want to go to the ocean with you," he whispered.

"You can't," she said. "The ocean is mine, and you have things of your own to do."

"But maybe," he struggled to say, "Maybe I can come there when I'm done."

"You'll never be done."

"I think I love you, Janeane."

She squeezed him. "You are beautiful, Prophet. You can come to my sea whenever you want. It's right here." She kissed his forehead again. "Always."

He opened his eyes and was alone, but her scent was still heavy in the room.

◄►► ◄◄►

Jane and Broken sat across from one another. Jane held Ian in her lap. He gurgled happily; he obviously liked her.

"Have... have you seen anyone else?" Jane asked hesitantly.

"Sky Ranger a few times, from far away," Broken said.

"Did... did they try to find you? Did the LED come after you?"

Broken shook her head. "No. You?"

"They... no. They didn't." Jane cradled Ian in her arms. "Do you miss it?"

Broken closed her eyes, a million emotions warring inside her. How could she answer that question?

"What does she do?"

"Who?"

"Janeane! Who else?"

"She works for the CA. I thought you knew that." Monica tossed a crust of bread to the ducks, who gobbled it up greedily. One duck, a big black and white male, was muscling all the other ducks out of the area, so no one else could eat. It was January, but the ducks had stayed. Strange. Michael and Monica tried to throw the food to the others, but the big one kept grabbing it away. "That duck's a jerk."

"What does she do at the CA?" The Colonization Authority controlled everything that went to and came back from the twenty or so worlds humanity had colonized.

"Oh, she just deals with transportation issues," Monica said vaguely. "I worry about her there. The CA isn't safe."

"Why not?"

Monica stared at him. "Don't you know? I thought you were a political artist or something."

"Right. I, um, specialized."

Monica rolled her eyes. "The Reformists hate them. One of the first things they did was expose so-called corruption at the CA." She scowled. "They're jealous of the power it has."

"If they're so powerful, they should be able to take care of themselves."

"When the UNP was in charge, they could," Monica said. "Not anymore." The UNP was the United Nations Party, recently kicked out of power by the Reformists after fifty years. "I'm a UNP member. So is Janeane. I worry sometimes..."

"Janeane will be safe," Michael said. "No matter what."

"Yeah," Monica said. "But what about us?"

Michael couldn't answer her.

[CHAPTER 9]

THE OTHERS WERE ALL GATHERED IN A tense clot around a screen in the common room when they returned.

"What happened?" Monica asked, worry choking her voice.

"President Lin escaped," Andrew told her, expressionless. "Some party members got her out of jail." President Lin Su-Kwan had been the president of the Confederation before Damien Peltan. She'd been put in prison by the Reformists, Michael knew, but he wasn't sure why.

"Isn't that good?" Monica said.

Lydia shook her head. "You'll see."

The reports took an ominous tone. A government spokesman came on to announce that the United Nations Party leadership had been behind the breakout.

He said that the government would "take direct action against an outlaw party."

"'Outlaw party?' The UNP? What does that mean?" Monica seemed genuinely confused.

"It means we were right about them," Lydia said bitterly. She took off the small UNP pin she'd been wearing since Michael had first met her, and put it in her pocket. Everyone watched her, agog.

Monica went to the kitchen, and Michael followed her.

"What's going on?"

Monica looked like she was ready to cry. "Lydia was on the UNP committee for our district. I wanted to join it next year. Can the administration really do this? We were the Confederation government for fifty years! How can we be traitors?"

Michael thought. "I don't know," he admitted. "But didn't President Lin do something like try to steal the election? Um. I mean, isn't that why they put her in jail."

Monica glared at him. "Yeah, they *say* she did. But she didn't. We believe Peltan really took over the government in a military coup." She stared at him. "How could you miss that?"

"Other priorities," Michael said. Joe had been sick and dying in 2105. They shared an uncomfortable silence for a few minutes, then rejoined the others in the living room.

An hour later, the police caught up with Lin and her compatriots on the wide plains of central Australia. The wind whipped up dust all around. In the center, stepping gingerly out of an open-top car, was Lin herself. A group

of Black Bands—not the police after all—in smart uniforms surrounded her. She raised a hand—a feeble old
woman, all of five feet tall, raised a hand to surrender—

The Black Bands opened fire. Lin Su Kwan fell, disappearing into the dust.

Lydia screamed.

An hour after that, President Peltan declared martial law. He also declared that all opposition parties had
been outlawed, because of suspected terrorist ties.

Riots broke out all over the world. The news reports framed it as evidence: the opposition was bent on
disorder and chaos.

"What's going to happen to us now?" Andrew
wondered.

"We're fucked," Shawn said evenly. He seemed no
more or less disturbed than before.

Horror flooded Michael.

—Fire...
—The ocean...

He smiled and sighed. He looked around for Janeane, but found she wasn't there. She hadn't come back
from work yet.

"Where's Janeane?" he asked.

Monica turned white. "The CA! They'll take it over!
They'll kill her!"

The Colonization Authority was a symbol of the old
regime. The Reformists hated it. And they had just seen

what the Reformists did to things they hated.

A frenzy of activity gripped the *rhi*. They called her office; she wasn't there. Later, they watched the screen in horror as the Black Bands stormed the Colonization Authority transfer station in Newark... but Janeane wasn't one of the prisoners taken, nor was she listed among the dead. No one had seen her.

"Janeane can take care of herself," Lydia said absently, after a while. "Don't worry about her. She'll come home."

She didn't.

And yet Michael still held the ocean in his mind. Behind the peaceful waves, though, an urgent need to be gone was building.

They watched the reports for a while longer, and then decided, fitfully, to go to bed. A few riots had broken out in Manhattan and Brooklyn, but nothing had spread their way yet. Supposedly Australia was going insane. Janeane still hadn't come back.

Michael paced sleeplessly around the house for an hour, unable to go to his room, unable even to think. Janeane had to be safe. Maybe she had gone to her ocean.

He paled.

—Fire.

Janeane was out of the house tonight.

He rushed back to his room and bundled his few possessions and some cash into his pack. He almost didn't notice the envelope on the pillow, but the pale blue paper caught his attention as he turned to go. He opened it.

A letter. He read it quickly.

Time to leave, Prophet. These are for you.
All my love. Godspeed.

Three pieces of paper fluttered to the ground.

Tickets. To Valen. Each bore the CA stamp, and each had two hundred credits taped to it.

"Thank you, Janeane," he whispered, and ran out of the room, putting the envelope and its precious contents in the inside pocket of his jacket.

He ran to Broken's room, but she was already up. She held Ian in her arms.

"Time to go?" she asked.

He nodded. "How did you get him away from Jane?"

"She fell asleep. I hold him every night when she sleeps."

Off in the distance, they could hear shouting. Had the mob come already?

"We have to go *now*," Michael said urgently.

But guilt held him in place. He had to try.

"Help me," he said. He banged on Lydia's door. "Wake up! Mob! Get out, now! Now!"

Broken caught on. They ran around the circle of the house, banging on doors. "Wake up! Mob!"

People stumbled out into the hallway, rubbing their eyes.

"What is this?" Andrew said. "Mike, what's happening?"

"A mob is coming," Michael said. "They will burn the house down."

"Of all the nonsense," Lydia said. "This house is fireproof. Isn't it, Andrew?"

Andrew turned red. "Sure. Sure, it is. I built it that way."

Michael seethed. *Cheap bastard. He didn't and he can't admit it.*

"They're coming tonight," he said. "You have to go."

"Nothing on the screens about it," deep-voiced Shawn growled. "No mob near here. We're safe. Go back to bed."

"I looked outside," Jane added. "Nothing. Michael, are you all right?"

"You're all in danger!" Michael said, getting hysterical. "Please, listen! I can see the future, I know it's going to happen *tonight!* Please!"

To his shock, Andrew laughed. "Oh, Mike, it's been a hard day. And we're all worried about Janeane. But we're safe! I promise."

Michael scanned each of their faces in turn.

—*Flames, flames...fire...*

Unavoidable. There were no other endings for any of them.

"Burn, then," he spat, scared and disgusted, and turned his back on them. Broken followed without saying a word.

Monica met them at the back door. He spun away,

not wanting to see her future set aflame.

"Take me with you," she said softly. Her jet-black hair was a mess, and she looked like she'd been crying. She wore a pack on her back. "Please. I believe you. Janeane left me a note, explaining. She... she knew things, too. So I figure you must be right. Please?"

He had three tickets.

One for him. One for Ian. One for Broken.

One for Monica? There weren't enough. Still. *Still.*

He nodded. "All right. Come on."

The four of them set off into the harsh winter night.

They struck north, away from the riots. Half an hour later, as they crested a hill by the bank of the frozen Hudson, Monica dared to look back.

The neighborhood where they had lived was a sea of flame.

Broken put her arm around the young woman and led her away, as tears ran down both of their cheeks.

Michael glanced at Monica. Her future was bound to theirs now. They walked down the hill as Ian moaned softly in the cold. The moon, silvery and uncaring, shone overhead.

[CHAPTER 10]

THE STREETS NORTH OF NEW YORK were mobbed with people fleeing the carnage in the city.

"What's happening?" Michael asked a man with three children and a pack full of belongings slung on his back.

"Black Bands are torching entire neighborhoods," he gasped, struggling under his heavy load. "Anyone with a UNP registration is getting hauled in."

"Is anyone fighting back?" Monica asked.

The man sighed. "Yeah. They're getting killed. Black Bands were ready for 'em."

"I saw six cops turn on the Black Bands," a younger man said. "They got shot, too. But *cops* are fightin' 'em."

"Good," a woman whispered viciously. "I hope they all die."

"Which?" someone asked her. "Cops or Black Bands?"

"*All* of them."

Michael nodded. He'd seen this sort of day in some people's futures. Many of them had been police or Black Bands.

They blended in with the crowd, just four more refugees heading north. Several times along the way, they saw squads of Black Bands keeping watch over the road. Vehicles carrying more Black Bands and even some Army troops passed through the crowds, heading south towards the fighting. They could hear, from time to time, the roar of aircraft overhead.

Morning dawned, cold and miserable. Michael felt like he had been walking for most of his life. Ian had stopped crying, but Michael could tell his diaper was wet, and he was probably badly chafed. There was nothing he could do. If he stopped, what would happen? Better to keep moving.

There was an empty lot where refugees camped, warmed by fires started in old metal trash barrels. Michael, Monica, and Broken sat together, as close to one of the barrels as they could get. Michael put a fresh diaper on Ian, leaving the old one where it fell.

Someone had brought a portable media screen, and set it up near where they were huddled. Almost all of the refugees turned to watch. A stunningly beautiful woman, wearing a serious expression, sat at a desk, reading the latest news.

"...Continuing coverage of the terrorist uprising in New York, where it is reported that traitorous police, loyal to the now-banned UNP, have been engaging the

Civil Guard"—apparently they were calling the Black Bands the Civil Guard now—"and the military in sporadic fighting in the city's residential areas. It is believed that the terrorists are attempting to use the population as human shields. We urge citizens to do everything they can to cooperate with government forces, or just to remain as safe as possible." Pictures of fighting flashed on the screen. "Military sources say that our government has reclaimed most of the city from the terrorists, and that the last few nests should be wiped out shortly." More pictures of heroic-looking soldiers and Black Bands appeared.

Broken gasped. There was a flying man wearing the uniform of the Black Bands.

"Extrahuman Union leader Sky Ranger, who recently added his organization to the long list of Civil Guard Reserves, helped to contain the terrorist threat," the gorgeous woman said.

Sky Ranger looked directly into the camera. "Any sort of violence against the lawfully elected government is illegal, and morally wrong. I urge anyone who is still fighting to put down your weapons. You will be treated well."

The announcer nodded. "Thank you, Sky Ranger. And here's a look at today's weather—"

Michael turned away. Not a word about the Black Bands torching neighborhoods. Nothing about UNP members being arrested. Or murdered.

Broken was sitting quietly. "How *could* he?" she asked no one in particular.

"That son of a bitch Sky Ranger," someone nearby growled. "I saw him blasting away at a position manned by old men and boys. Some fucking hero."

A murmur of tired agreement rippled through the crowd, then subsided.

Broken shook her head. "He's a good man," she muttered. "A good man. A good man." She patted her cloak. "Where's my bottle? Where's my booze? Did I leave it?" She kept muttering and swearing to herself for a while. No one responded.

Gossip and rumor started to spread through the camp.

"Peltan's dead," one person insisted. "My brother in Australia told me."

"Lin is still alive," said another. "She's fighting with the rebels now."

Others were more realistic. "The UNP is fighting in Western Australia. Supposedly they have control of Perth."

"No, they're basing themselves out of Sydney."

"I heard there's a war up in space."

"Half the colonies have seceded! My father says so."

"The Rätons have invaded," another said. This caused a hush. "They have Mantillies and Quela, and are heading for Earth now."

"Says who?"

"My friend says he heard it from a Black Band."

A heated argument followed. Was it better to live under Peltan, or the Rätons? Humans had been allies with the Rätons before, during the long Rogarian War. That was twenty-five years in the past, though. What would the Rätons be like now? No one could agree.

Everyone was starting to get hungry. "Where's the government?" cried more than one person. "Why don't they feed their people?"

"Maybe they really are gone," a few whispered. "Maybe the government fell, and we're on our own."

Michael knew that none of the rumors were true.

An oldtimer sighed. "It was like this during the Last War, too," he told Michael and anyone else who would listen. "I was a boy then, but things don't change."

Michael saw Monica reach into her pack.

"What are you doing?" He was next to her in a flash.

"Getting some food," she said. A few heads turned her way.

"Not here. You want to start another riot? Come on. We should keep moving."

"Why? Look, I'm hungry. Ian's hungry, too. I bet you didn't bring any formula."

"Just trust me," Michael said. "Let's go. Quietly. This place isn't safe."

"*Why* should I trust you? *Fuck* you!" She buried her head in her arms. "My family is *dead*. They're all dead. Jane, Andrew, Lydia, Fred, Shawn—Oh, God! They can't be—" She sobbed uncontrollably. Michael, not knowing what else to do, put an arm around her.

"We should go," Broken said.

"I know," Michael said helplessly. "But we can wait a few minutes."

A phalanx of Black Bands showed up about half an

hour later. They had bread and water, which they tossed in huge packages down to the crowd. People scrambled to get what they could.

Michael tried to restrain Broken from leaping into the fray, but couldn't stop her. She returned a few minutes later with six loaves of bread, a split lip, a black eye, and a huge grin on her face. Monica watched in horrified fascination as Broken's lip repaired itself.

"Jesus," she said.

"It's something she can do," Michael explained lamely.

"I wish I could do that," Monica said.

"Me, too," agreed Michael. Ian started crying. "Can he eat bread?"

"Does he have any teeth?" Monica asked.

"No."

"Then probably not."

They ate some of the bread, staying put despite Broken's repeated demands to leave. Michael wanted to press onward, too, but he was so tired...

"What are *they* doing?" Monica wanted to know. Soldiers, along with a few Black Bands, had taken up positions around the perimeter of the camp and were now simply standing there, watching the crowd.

Michael looked at them. Their possibilities came in vague flashes; nothing specific or useful came to him. "No idea. Maybe we *should* go."

"Yeah," said Monica.

"Right," Broken agreed. "Time to go."

At the edge of the camp, an armed Black Band stopped them. "Where are you going? Do you have identification?"

"ID was lost when the house was set on fire," Michael said. "Sorry. We're going to go to her sister's place in, uh, Danbury."

The Black Band did a quick search of their packs. He took some of the food they'd been carrying and passed it out to his friends. He examined the pack of thin diapers closely, and decided he didn't want it. Michael tried not to think about about the money and tickets from Janeane he had strapped to his leg. "Go ahead," the Black Band said at last.

They went without complaint. What else was there to do?

They joined a stream of refugees heading further north. A few had vehicles, now, and were carrying people anywhere they could fit them. Men, women, and children clung to the sides, roof, trunk, and even underneath any vehicle that passed by, if just to get momentary relief from walking.

Michael asked everyone he could about the latest news. New York was mostly back in the government's hands, but the riots and arrests hadn't stopped. Anyone who had ever been associated with the UNP was leaving, quickly.

But where was there for them to go? Refugee camps had sprouted all over Westchester, but most of these were being guarded by Black Bands and the Army. What would happen when the Black Bands decided to see who was who? Michael didn't want to be around for it. No more refugee camps, he informed Monica and Broken. They didn't object.

⊲⊳⊲⊳

They weren't entirely certain where they were going. Michael's prescience didn't help one bit. He was blind to the future, for now, driven only by the need to go southwest to Delmarva. Media screens, usually plastered to the sides of buildings, spewed news at them. New York was still unsafe. Fighting still raged, but the government was winning. The government had mopped up all but the worst of the cells. The streets were still too dangerous; citizens had been told in no uncertain terms to stay inside.

There was very little news from the rest of the planet, or from the twenty or so other worlds that made up the Confederation.

Little by little, the refugees dropped away, herded into camps by newly arrived Confederation soldiers and local Black Bands. Each time the soldiers or the thugs who looked like soldiers beckoned, Michael, Monica, and Broken walked on. No one stopped them.

They passed the Bush Tunnel, which ran under the Tappan Zee. The entrances were guarded by Black Bands in armored vehicles. They kept walking. There were other bridges, other tunnels.

Ian was crying, but they had little food to give him. Monica mashed up some bread and watered it down; he could swallow this, but he obviously didn't like it. He was much harder to carry, by now; he had gained a good deal of weight under Jane's care.

From time to time, they saw flights of hundreds

of small flying craft—flitters, fighters, and wingers, all heading for the city. They had come far enough not to be able to hear the dull thud of explosions, or the sharp staccato of gunfire.

"I wonder," Monica said. "I wonder what will happen tomorrow?"

"Who knows?" Michael said with a shrug.

She looked sharply at him. "Aren't you supposed to know the future? That's what Janeane said. That's what you told us. Can't you just *tell* me what's going to happen?"

He shook his head. "No, sorry. It doesn't really work that way." He took a deep breath. "What I do, is I look at someone's face. I have to look directly, or it doesn't work. That's why I look down a lot."

"I hadn't noticed," Monica said.

"Well, I do," said Michael, a little chagrined. "I don't want to see everything that's going to happen to everybody."

"Why not?" Monica asked. "Aren't you curious?"

"Go crazy," Broken snorted.

Michael nodded. "Yeah. Go crazy."

"Knew a guy," Broken said. "He could read minds. Didn't take nothin' to look and see what was on someone's mind. Had to try hard to keep thoughts *out*. Told me people think about sick things, all the time, every day. Everybody's crazy, he said. But who knows? Just him."

"What happened to him?" Monica asked.

"Went to a colony," Broken said. "Bought a thousand acres of desert somewhere. Don't know which planet. Said he wanted to get away from everybody."

"Can't blame him," Michael said.

"Is it like that for you?" Monica asked.

"It's a little like that, but not quite so bad. There's so much information. I have to try and sort it out. When I look at someone, I see their possible futures."

"So you *can* see what will happen tomorrow," Monica said.

"Not exactly," Michael admitted. "I see glimpses. Images. I don't see everything. I usually don't get surroundings or dates, just flashes. And it's not what *will* happen, just what *could*. At least that's how I understand it."

"Sucks," Broken said. "I used to fly. That's more fun."

[CHAPTER 11]

THE SUN CREPT UPWARDS, THEN BEGAN slipping down the sky's broad inner curve again. They had covered too many miles to count. Michael's feet were killing him. There were far fewer refugees on the road here; they had somehow veered off the main track, and onto a side road.

Now they were right by the river. Trees blossomed from the brown-red husks of ancient buildings; here and there an intact house glowed with electric life. But most houses along the road were long since abandoned. The forests of old New York were reclaiming what man had stolen.

"There used to be more people," Broken said. "But they all either died in the war or went to a colony." She remembered Sky Ranger telling her that. He seemed very sad when he said it. She never understood why.

Weren't the people on the colonies better off? And the people who were dead didn't feel anything at all.

"Joe said that Americans didn't want to be in their country anymore after we—they—lost the Last War," Michael said thoughtfully. "It was a sin to be an American. Joe said that we—Americans—used to be very proud."

"Who was Joe?" asked Monica.

"A friend of my father," said Michael. "He raised me, mostly."

Broken didn't remember her father. Had she ever had one? Yes, she must have. She wondered what he had looked like. Somehow, she kept seeing Sky Ranger—not the one who flew above New York now (don't think about what he's doing, she told herself firmly)—but the old one. The one she had known as a little girl; the old man Sky Ranger inherited his title from. She'd met him when the Union first took her in.

Before that point... she had no memories at all save one.

There was endless water all around her. No... behind her was soft sand, sharp rocks. Further out, mighty walls of water crashed into the continent. She looked down into the salty water of the tidepool. A strange face waved and jumped atop the shifting sea. Behind it, something small scuttled past.

She reached in to pluck it out, but it caught her and pulled with all its might.

"_____!" she called. (Who could she be calling to?)

But no one came. The thing pulled again, and she disappeared underwater.

"Now," said the beast, "you belong to me." It had a thousand tentacles, and one giant mouth.

She screamed.

Michael and Monica stared at her.

"B?" Monica held a hand out. "Are you okay?"

Broken nodded. She was on her back, lying in the road.

She needed to stop remembering. She could do that. She needed a drink.

A light snow began to fall as night blanketed the empty land. All four of them shivered—even Ian, wrapped snugly in his blanket, quivered and wailed mournfully.

"We need to find shelter," Michael said, looking at Monica and Broken. "This is going to be a big storm. We don't want to be caught in it."

"You predict that?" Monica asked.

"Yes," Michael said. "Just now, looking at you."

But no places of shelter made themselves apparent.

"Keep walking," Michael said grimly. "Keep walking."

Monica snapped, "You predict *that*? Did you predict a place to get out of the snow? You predict anything *useful*?"

"Shut up," Michael growled. They walked faster,

despite their aching feet.

Then, below, on the riverbank, they saw a swaying light. Michael could vaguely make out the shape of a man standing by it. It was a boat; the man stood on a short dock, untying it.

Michael was too far away to get a good read. He took the chance anyway. He was cold, and getting a little desperate. "Hey!" he yelled, waving his hands. "Hey!"

"What are you—?" Monica had time to ask before Michael broke into a run.

"Wait!" Michael called. "Please, wait!"

The man would never wait. Who would trust a stranger these days? There was a war going on in the city. Thugs in black uniforms patrolled the streets. Refugees lived like animals, and treated everyone else the same way.

But the man stopped and looked up.

"Wait, please!" Michael shouted again, skidding down the embankment. Monica and Broken waited with Ian on the high road.

Now he'll go. Now he'll cast off, and we'll be stuck here, Michael thought. Now. Now. Now.

He could have. The flickers of possibility Michael got from him suggested that he still might. But the man stayed put, patiently waiting for Michael to run up to him. "Wait, please. Please take us across. We have a baby."

"Take you across?" The man scratched his chin. "Hm. How many?"

"Four, including the baby," Michael said. "We have nowhere to go. We came from the city. Our house was burned."

The man's expression softened. "Come on, then,"

he said.

Michael beckoned. Monica had to help a suddenly reluctant Broken down the slope, while Michael rushed back to take Ian. They clambered into the wooden boat, and the old man untied the rope and shoved off from the dock. The boat glided smoothly out into the river.

"There's no motor," Monica said.

The old man grinned. "Boats aren't allowed on the river unless you have a pass and a license and some other such. But they don't see me if I don't use any power but my own." He picked up an oar and handed it to Michael. "Help me out, son," he said. Michael took it and sat next to him on the bench. "I don't usually have passengers, but put two at the oars and we go faster. We go on three. One-two-*three*. Like that. Put your oar in straight, and pull straight back. Got it?"

Michael nodded, not sure that he did.

"All right. Let me get us on the right track." The man put his oar in the water and pulled. The boat swung around to the right. They were facing the shore they had come from. The prow of the boat faced the far shore. "Okay, son, one-two-*three*. One-two-*three*."

Michael put his oar in and did his best to keep up. He tried to dip his oar in straight and pull straight back, as he'd been instructed. He didn't do it right at first, but got the hang of it about halfway through. Thankfully, the old man was very tolerant.

"Ever pulled an oar?" he asked as they worked. Michael shook his head. "Too bad. It's good for you. Put some muscle on you! People now never even think of it. Two-*three*. Good, you're getting it down!"

The old man didn't ask them any questions as they

glided across the river. It was eerily peaceful. The only sound came from the *thunk-splish* of the oars. Snow fell lightly all around them as evening deepened into night. Even Broken seemed transfixed by the silence. Michael's muscles ached, his back was sore, but he found himself hoping the trip would never end.

Eventually, though, they pulled up to a dock on the other side of the river; the current had pulled them far to the south, which seemed to be just fine with the old man. He leapt out onto the dock with astonishing spryness for his age and the amount of work he'd just done—Michael certainly didn't feel like jumping out of the boat. "Toss the rope," he ordered Michael, who found it and threw it to the old man. "Now let's get indoors."

It took them a moment to realize he was offering them the hospitality of his home. Michael was too tired to refuse, too tired to even check possible futures. They trudged wearily up a hill towards an old two-story house, almost certainly built long before the Last War. The porch light was lit invitingly, and the house was blessedly warm inside.

"Mary Ann!" he called. "Mary Ann, I'm back!"

A plump old woman, her face framed by a halo of white hair, peered from out of the kitchen. "Who are these?"

"Refugees from the city," he said.

She made a face and sighed. "All right. You can't help yourself. I'll make some more dinner."

"They can have mine," said the old man. "And yours, too. I'll cook us up some beans."

"But Will!"

He whispered something to her, and her expression changed. She looked down at the floor, then back up at Michael and his companions. "I'm sorry, you'll have to excuse me. Of course you're welcome. Please sit. I've made a meat stew."

Broken was looking all around the house, smelling the unfamiliar smells and running her hands over the wooden banister and table. "This place is so beautiful," she said. "Have I been here before?"

The woman put steaming hot stew into three bowls on the table. She took Ian, rocking him in her arms.

Michael sat. "Thank you very much," he said, trying to be as polite as he could. "You didn't have to help us—"

"Of course we did," the woman—Mary Ann—said. "In '46, we were on the road, too. We were kids then, of course. But the Chinese and the Europeans bombed our town, then sent their soldiers. We had to run."

"It was just the Europeans bombed," said the man. Will.

"Right, right. But some of the soldiers were Chinese," said Mary Ann. "This was east of here, in Connecticut. So we know what it's like."

"How's New York?" asked the old man. "We don't turn on the screen much."

"Let him eat," Mary Ann hushed him.

"No, I don't mind," said Michael, and related some of what he knew and had heard about the city's uprising and quick fall. "Our house was burned. Black Bands."

"Those dirty thugs," Mary Ann said sadly, shaking her head. "A neighbor of ours has a son with them. I never knew a crueler young man."

"Times are hard now," Will agreed. "And they'll be hard for a while."

"Probably," said Michael, who knew.

"Thank you for the soup," Monica said timidly.

"You're welcome, dear. And aren't you a pretty young thing! Such eyes. What's your name?"

"I'm Monica," she said. "This is Michael and B."

"Bea," repeated Mary Ann. "Lovely name. I haven't heard it in ages."

"Baby's Ian," Broken said. "He's not any of ours."

"Well, I figured that." Mary Ann said. It was sort of obvious—Ian's skin was several shades darker than any of theirs. Michael couldn't figure out why people kept asking.

"He's sort of mine," Michael interjected hastily. "I agreed to take care of him before his mother died."

"Oh, the poor thing!" Mary Ann kissed him on top of his head. Ian yelped in surprise. "Poor little orphan. Poor baby! Well, your Uncle Michael will take care of you, isn't that right?" She beamed at Michael, who turned red. "Well, we're Will and Mary Ann Brown. You can stay here the night, until this snow clears up."

"Thank you," Michael and Monica said together.

Will held up a hand. "Don't even mention it. You're welcome here."

Beside him, Michael felt Monica start to shake. She put her hands over her eyes and started to quietly sob to herself.

"Her family," Michael explained. The old couple nodded. What more needed to be said? Mary Ann came over and put an arm around Monica's shoulder as she poured out her grief.

◆►◄◆

They ate their fill, then went straight to the beds Mary Ann had made for them upstairs. Monica remained for a while, then came to join them.

Michael drifted off to sleep thinking he had arrived in Heaven.

When he woke the next morning, the world outside had turned white. A dazzling blue sky capped the endless plains of snow. Mary Ann had cups of strong coffee ready for them downstairs. Will had already taken the boat across the river to sell some fresh eggs and knick-knacks they made at a local market—Mary Ann figured other refugees would buy them. "He'd better not give them away. But he will. I know him," she said, shaking her head, but smiling as she said it.

"Tastes good," Broken said, slurping her coffee down greedily.

"This is a nice place," Monica said wistfully. "I grew up in the city."

"Oh, so did Will and I," Mary Ann said. "Had our children there. But we always wanted to move out here, so we did, thirty years back. Now Will has his land and his boat, and I keep chickens out back."

"You're lucky," said Michael.

"No luck about it," Mary Ann replied proudly. "We earned every square inch. I was a veterinarian. I took care of people's sick poodles all my life. He was an engineer for a large company, doing rebuilding work after the War." She took a long sip of coffee. "He even went to war against the Rogarians, when that came, because of his mechanical knowledge. They taught him a bit about starships. Fortunately for us, it's all out of date, now. They can't make him go back."

As they made ready to leave, Michael thanked Mary Ann again, and made her promise to thank Will.

"No trouble." She had washed their clothes, and gave them some woolen caps to wear in the cold. Michael tried to give her some of the money Janeane had left him, but she refused.

"Don't mention it. But if we get a hundred like you, we might start to have charging. Now get going."

She loaded them up with some food and other items, and sent them out into the snow. When they had trudged away from the house, Michael opened the envelope she'd pressed into his hand last. A twenty-credit bill was there.

"Good people," Broken said. "Rare." She pulled out a clear glass bottle from her coat and took a long pull from it.

"Broken!" said Michael, aghast. "Did you steal that?"

She didn't bother to acknowledge him, but smiled up at the sky.

[CHAPTER 12]

IT WASN'T EASY GOING; FEW SURFACE
roads beyond the main ones were well-maintained anymore, and even fewer than that were plowed. Worse,
they had to constantly squint against the white glare of
the noonday sun off the new-fallen snow. They chunked
through the snowfields, feet and faces numb, until they
reached the outskirts of a town.

Its citizens were prepared for what they thought
might be coming. Windows were boarded up, and signs
reading "No Food Here" and "Keep Going to Next Town
2km" were hung over doors. Still, about a dozen aim-
less-looking refugees milled around on the street, looking for something to eat or do.

They found only one building open; the town library. "Let's go in and get warm," Monica suggested,
seeing several other ragged travelers heading in. Mi-

chael agreed, and Broken followed wearily along.

Michael and Monica took Ian off to change his diaper, which was beginning to sag ominously. Broken separated from the clot of other refugees warming up in the library's main foyer and went off to wander the stacks.

At once, she felt a sense of peace overwhelming her.

Libraries were a thing of the past, and Sky Ranger had been fascinated by them. He had taken her to the New York Public Library, an ancient building miraculously left unscathed by bombs and neglect.

"Hundreds of thousands of books were kept in libraries in each little city and town, all across the continent," he said.

"Wow," Silverwyng muttered, singularly unimpressed. She'd rather be flying than get dragged through a musty old library.

"All of the greatness of the older generations is here," Sky Ranger intoned. "For us, it's only a matter of finding and implementing it. Our society is so corrupt. We've become so close to aliens, to outer space and the future that we've forgotten Earth and the past."

"Yeah," Silverwyng said, surprising herself by half agreeing with him. Suddenly the place seemed a little less musty—more peaceful.

She had secretly come back to the library more than a dozen times before leaving the Union, and was often there after. She rarely read the books. She just liked the atmosphere.

<>► ◄<>

Broken ran her hand along the spines of books, and plucked one out at random.

Extrahumans: The 2091 Guide.

What? There was a section on Extrahumans? She started to put the book back, then thought better of it. She opened it gingerly, and saw photo after photo of faces she knew.

Crimson Cadet, so brave and funny. Duskman and Clatter, always together (probably lovers, Sky Ranger had said). Strong Rex and Mr. Invincible, lifting weights and posing. Triggerfinger, Armor Pete, Chainmail, Ladybird...

Each member of the Law Enforcement Division of the Union had his or her own page, with a big glossy photo and "statistics," relating to cases solved, criminals captured, that sort of thing.

She gasped. "Doctor Lucky Jane," the caption read. Jane smiled winsomely. "A new addition to the Law Enforcement Division of the Extrahuman Union, she has phenomenal good fortune. She is a wise surgeon and sure to make an impact."

Dead, now. Broken tried not to think of that.

Nearer the back was a listing of all the other Union members, those who hadn't joined the LED. There was a little square picture of each one, with his or her name and the "extra-human" ability he or she had.

Yes. Near the end.

"Silverwing: Flight, healing."

She studied at the fading picture of a young, thin-faced girl with shockingly silver hair. How old had she been? Fourteen, maybe? It was before she had started spelling her name differently, so she had to be younger than sixteen.

Even then, she couldn't remember the year she was born, exactly, or what her parents had looked like. The Union had come for her at too young an age.

She flipped back to Jane's picture. "Poor Lucky," Broken said, and replaced the book neatly on the shelves. She found she couldn't call forth the kind of grief that Monica had shown. Not right now.

She scanned the shelves, suddenly hungry for more. Dozens of books flew into her hands, dozens more she cast aside.

She sat at a table, poring over the past, repeating sentences to herself out loud.

"The Extrahuman Union was formed in response to growing public unease regarding the small population of Extrahumans or 'superheroes,'" she read. "They began to be noticed by the population and by world governments in the 2030s, but the trauma of the Last War and the formation of the Confederation precluded any action before 2053, when the Union was founded. A young hero named Sky Ranger was its first leader."

The very first Sky Ranger, the great hero who had fought the Rogarians during their aborted invasion of human space in the 2060s. There had been two more after him, including the one she had shared the sky with so long ago.

She picked up a different book.

"Superhumans or 'Extrahumans' are not trusted by the people as a whole," she read. "In fact, their powers are the object of great envy and hatred."

She put that book down, and picked up another.

"'Extrahuman' is a nicer way of saying 'mutant,' although not so glamorous as saying 'superhuman' or, more popularly, 'superhero.' In and of itself, it is a word that means very little."

Yet another book.

"The Confederation Government mandated that all 'Extrahumanoids' be members of the new Union. All those who did not wish to join were tracked down by those who already had. Many died defending what they saw as their liberty."

She shuddered. She'd had to do that. There had been a man who could create fire. He had lived out in the woods, by himself. A hiker had seen him starting a small cooking fire, and had reported him to the Union.

When they came for him, he stood his ground. They'd been forced to tear him apart to stop him from incinerating the whole team. It had been a ghastly business.

She'd questioned that day whether or not she really belonged with the LED. In the end, though, it didn't matter.

Flip, flip.

"Evidence suggests that the government uses Extrahumans for its own ends. Several have disappeared with little to no explanation... Silverwyng, for example."

She let out a solitary, hollow laugh and picked up another book.

"Why don't Extrahumans have names? Real names, I mean. Why the strange titles? Do they even have regular names? What do they call one another?"

Broken thought about that. She'd never had a "real" name, not one she could remember.

"Hey, kiddo!" called the woman. "Come on, you'll be late!"

She poked the water, and the crabs scuttled away. Except for a big blue one, which drew nearer...

She paged to another chapter.

"Extrahumans are not free citizens," she read. "They either chain themselves to their Union, or are forced into it. Many are brought to the Union as children. The Union is not supposed to be controlled by the government, but it is. How many times have the actions of the Extrahumans and the aims of the government neatly coincided?"

She picked up the last book, which was far smaller than the others, nearly a pamphlet.

"Extrahumans, supermen, mutants, whatever you call them: They are dangerous. Their very existence threatens humanity. Their shameless collaboration with a corrupt government and a corrupt party aligns them irrevocably with the oppressors of free will in our state. They are a danger that must be dealt with."

In horror, she dropped the book to the table. Who would hate her so? She glanced at the author's name and gasped.

Damien Peltan, now President of the Confederation. He had written the book nearly fifteen years before, when he was just an angry young partisan.

She shivered a little and reached inside her cloak. She'd drained dry the bottle she'd lifted from the nice people. What would happen now? She pushed the books away, leaned back in her chair, and, against her will, remembered...

[CHAPTER 13]
-PAST-

A LITTLE GIRL SAT ON THE STEPS OF the vast skyscraper in which all the men and women who had some sort of abnormal ability were housed, crying bitterly.

An older boy came to sit next to her. She knew him, of course. He was called Little Hawk now, but the rumors had started to fly around that he might soon be the new Sky Cadet. The old one had died in a fall only weeks before, much to his guardian's distress. Sky Ranger hadn't spoken to anyone since.

The boy, perhaps soon to be heir to the entire Union, walked with the easy, confident swagger of someone who has never wanted for much.

"Why are you crying? Do you miss your parents?"

"I don't remember them," the girl sobbed. "I can't even remember my name!"

"Your name is Silverwing," he said calmly. "That's what your badge says."

"But it—it isn't *really* my name," she managed, sniffling. "I can't remember what my momma called me... I have to think..." She started crying again.

The boy put his arm around her. "Don't cry. Your old name meant nothing. It was just words. *My* name was Robbie. But I don't care—it doesn't mean what Little Hawk does. And whatever your old name was, it isn't as good as Silverwing."

She wasn't really reassured, but she wanted Little Hawk to like her, so she tried to stop crying to show him he'd helped. After a few sniffles and hiccups, the tears slowed. "You really think so?"

"I like Silverwing," he said. "Did you make it up?"

She shook her head. "Triad did."

He nodded. "She likes making names. She does a good job. She did Crimson Cadet's. His is *really* cool."

She agreed that it was. Everyone envied Crimson Cadet. He was big, good-looking, and fun to be around.

"How long have you been here?" Little Hawk asked.

"Three years," she said, feeling the tears well up in her again. She tried to fight them back.

"That's not too long. Maybe you'll feel better in a while. Hey, what can you do? I can fly, and I have extra strength and speed."

She smiled, a genuine smile this time. "I fly, too."

"Want to go fly for a bit?"

She shook her head, surprised. "We're not allowed!"

He grinned cockily. "I can do whatever I want. Who'll punish me for it? C'mon. Race you to the top of the tower."

"Okay." She stood and lifted herself a few inches off the ground. He did likewise.

"Ready? Go!" They arced upwards, twisting and whirling around the edges of the tower.

Silverwing was easily twice as fast as Little Hawk; she saw it immediately. She checked her speed a little, letting him keep up. She glanced over at him, and saw a look of incredible strain and concentration on his face. It looked like flying for him was *work*. She flew without effort.

He touched the top of the tower a split second before she did. "Yeah!" he called out to the sky. "Yaaaaah!" He beamed at her. "You're good."

She shivered with delight. Supposedly, Little Hawk was one of the fastest fliers. Not even bearded, mysterious Sky Ranger could quite outmatch him. Was she so much faster than anyone else? She smiled secretly and looked down. Below was the street, separated from the tower by a high steel fence. Only a slim, covered walkway connected them to the outside world.

But who could control the sky? The world lay open before her, the clouds beckoning. Who would stop her if she decided to leave?

She had a vague feeling that she ought to fly south, maybe towards a beach. But what was there? Who would she recognize? She drifted slowly to the ground, thirty stories below, peeking in windows as she passed. Inside, children learned, LED members trained, doctors studied charts and diagrams, and people simply lived. The Tower was a world unto itself. There was no need to go outside. No need at all...

Dimly, she had the feeling that she was a prisoner here. But it didn't matter. As long as she could fly, everything was all right.

The boy did not float down after her. He was looping around the spire of the Tower, yelling and whooping with sheer joy. She saw a man in a trailing blue cape slip out an opening in the upper floors. He was old, with a white beard. He caught up to the boy, then flew around him. They circled one another, racing around the building, then speeding off together into the distance.

Who could doubt, now? Little Hawk would be Sky Cadet, and then Sky Ranger someday. He was the crown prince of the Union. No one would punish him.

Not so for Silverwing. Triad was waiting for her when she got back to her room. Three weeks of dishroom duty was now hers, for flying without permission.

Flip... flip...
Broken's memory, like the leaves of a book, fluttered back and forth in the wind.

Crimson Cadet was covered in blood. "What happened?" Silverwyng demanded, clutching his arm.

"He—he was shot," Sky Ranger said, face ashen. "While we were assisting the CA police, they *shot* him!"

"Who shot him?"

Crimson Cadet moaned. Dark red blood mixed with the orange-red of his outfit.

"The CA cops did!" Sky Ranger wailed. "I don't know why!"

He flew from the room, knocking down everything and everyone in his path.

Strong Rex had been there, too. "It isn't a lie," he said. "The Colonization Authority's cops called us to help them bust some smugglers. But it was an ambush. Sky and me got out of the way. But Crim got shot. We had to go back to get him."

It would come out later that the CA had taken bribes from several large criminal rings to take out some of the Extrahumans. But Sky Ranger wouldn't find that out until later. When he did, he would be furious.

I was supposed to go on that patrol, Silverwyng thought. But she hadn't. Her powers were so erratic, she wasn't allowed to fly anywhere. Sky Ranger, Doc, and Lucky all had forbidden it. So Crimson Cadet had gone in her place, and now here he lay, bleeding. It figured. They could have shot Silverwyng all they liked. She would heal. Crimson Cadet wouldn't.

He coughed up blood and called out, delirious. Doc worked furiously, Lucky at his side. Lucky seemed frantic, almost to the point of dementia. "Come on," she was muttering. "This should work." Even Doc seemed rattled.

"Crimson—" Silverwyng began to say.

"*Jack!*" he cried.

They stared at him, speechless.

"My name is Jack," he said, calm now, a smile blooming on his face. "I remember it now."

And he died, smiling still.

Lucky ran her hands over him in disbelief. "No,"

she murmured. "No. No."

"Crim?" Strong Rex whispered, then burst into tears.

"No," Lucky repeated. "I can't lose him. I don't lose people."

Later, she would collapse in Silverwyng's arms, moaning, "I never lost a patient! Ever! What's happening to me, Sil?" Silverwyng had no answers. Her own abilities were failing her. What reassurance could she offer?

Silverwyng wanted to go after Sky Ranger, but found her feet were rooted to the floor.

"Not now!" she cried. "Fly!" She ran and threw herself into the air, but crashed to the ground, sobbing hysterically. "Fly... I'm not broken... I can fly..." she repeated, over and over, until she had lost all sense of the words.

Flip, flip, flip...

Head on the table, Broken did not sleep, but let her memories go where they would.

"You're sure?" Red Knight asked. He didn't seem convinced.

"Yeah!" Silverwyng said enthusiastically. "I could offer a lot to the team. I can fly *fast*, much faster than Sky Ca—Sky *Ranger*—and I can heal quickly. I can do a lot!"

Red Knight glowered at her. "You're sure this isn't because of our new Sky Ranger? He'll be head of the squad soon."

She nodded, caught, but not willing to show it.

"No. I really want to do this."

He frowned, but relented. "All right, then. But this isn't easy. We don't have time for people to shirk."

She broke into a grateful grin. "I understand! When do I report for training?"

"Three weeks; the 23rd, at nine in the morning. Crim and Sky will be leading the session. I expect you to act *professionally*." The huge, well-muscled man studied her. "Sil, this may not be the right line of work for you. You're too sensitive. This whole thing can get very... disturbing. I don't want you cracking up."

She stood her ground. "I'm stronger than I look. I won't crack."

Red Knight grunted in response. "We'll see. The 23rd at nine. See you there." She got up and left quickly, before he could change his mind.

Flip...

A beach... waves crashed ashore off in the distance.

She reached down to the tide pool... a crab the color of the endless sky reached back...

Flip... flip...

"I'll never trust the government again," Sky Ranger said grimly.

"It wasn't the government," Strong Rex said. "The CA is corrupt, yeah, but—"

"Crimson Cadet is dead because the government allows *them* to exist." His eyes burned with hatred. "I'll make them regret it."

Flip... flip... flip...

"I love you," Silverwyng whispered to him. They were making love, far above the roofs and treetops, where no one could see them. The moonlight illuminated his perfect body. She ran her hands over his chest, clenching her feet as he moved inside her.

He didn't say anything.

For a horrible second, he looked terrifying, half shadow, half reflected sunlight. His eyes... his eyes... they didn't seem human.

A trick of the light, she told herself later, for when she looked again, he was normal. Finished, he smiled down at her as they glided over the clouds, still joined together.

Flip...

Triad and Brick were giving the lesson. It was a special day; all the Union's children were gathered together. "The Union," said kind, ancient Brick, "was set up to be a place for everyone like us to belong. If it didn't exist, we'd have nowhere to go. People sometimes don't trust us. Can anyone imagine why?"

Crimson Cadet's voice boomed out. "They don't like us 'cause we're different. Right?"

Triad nodded. "That's true, Crim. It's a sad fact. But humans are like that."

"Not all humans," said Brick. She smiled sadly. "But many."

"They're jealous," said the first Sky Cadet, who sat between Crim and Little Hawk. "They just can't stand that we're so great, right?" He and Crimson Cadet were good friends. They slapped hands together. Little Hawk looked on, plainly jealous.

"Well, yes and no. Maybe that's part of it," old Sky Ranger said, stroking his white beard, as he entered the room. "But it's mostly just a distrust of what's different and strange. Crimson is right, and S.C. is right, as well. There are other reasons, too, but those are the main ones."

"What are the other reasons?" Valor asked. Silverwing didn't like Valor; he was too smart.

Sky Ranger didn't speak for a while. "Better to ask me that again, some other time," he said, clearly troubled. After the class was done, Sky Ranger took Valor aside and spoke with him for a long time.

Valor said later that Sky Ranger told him that he was afraid people associated the Union with the heavy-handedness and corruption of their government. "He said it's better that people hate the UNP, too, even though they're in charge. He said *especially* because they're in charge, and we're like the UNP in a way." Valor seemed to understand it. Silverwing didn't care.

Then everyone forgot all about it a week later when Sky Cadet came back from a late night bruised and bleeding. He had fallen off a roof, but forgot to fly. Silverwing, who flew down corridors instead of walking, couldn't imagine how that was possible. But he had, and soon he died despite everything Doc tried to save him.

Flip...

"Extrahumans," complained a young, impatient Sky Ranger bitterly. "Like we're something *extra*. Not really human. Just something *else* that the rest of them don't need."

"That's surprisingly insightful," sighed Doc.

Silverwyng said nothing. *Hurry up. I want to fly, I want to fly again,* she thought impatiently.

Flip... flip...

"You're wrong," said Crimson Cadet. "You can't

be paranoid all the time. And the Reform Party is bad news."

"I'll do as I like," Sky Ranger snapped. "Just because you don't *understand* the Party—"

"I understand 'em plenty! They're a bunch of fascists! I know *that* much. They want to tell you what to think!"

"Well," retorted Sky Ranger, "Maybe someone *ought* to tell people how to think. Then they won't make so many bad choices."

"You're an idiot," Crimson Cadet spat, storming out. Silverwyng, hovering at the window, held her breath. Sky Ranger looked directly at her.

"Go away, Sil," he commanded. She flew off, despondent.

Flip... flip... flip... flip...

"I can't do anything," Doc said. "I'm sorry."

"But..." whispered Silverwyng. "But... what do I do?"

Doc shrugged. "You can live a normal life here in the Tower, doing research, teaching... there are a lot of other things to do here."

"But *flying*—" Silverwyng started, and found she couldn't finish. She ran from the room, not caring. Sky Ranger stood in the atrium, lost in thought.

"Sky—" she began. "Sky?"

"Go away, Sil," he said shortly. "I need to be alone."

She pulled up short. "I can't fly."

"I don't care," he barked. "Get out of my sight!"

Silverwyng did not cry, but simply walked down to her room. She opened the window and, without a thought, jumped out. She pushed off, trying to gain as much distance as she could.

She landed just outside the fence, and died at once. Her rebellious body knitted itself back together, and she awoke in agony. She crawled to an alley and hid.

They would come for her. There was an implant in her shoulder; they could track her.

She had a knife. She gritted her teeth and sawed her arm off. She passed out twice before she was done, but the arm finally fell free. She blacked out again, and awoke with her new arm half finished.

Broken stood unsteadily, and clutched Silverwyng's arm in her hand. She threw it over the fence, back toward the Tower. With that, she walked off into the night.

◆►◄◆

Flip... flip... the book slammed shut.

Broken roused herself. Michael and Monica sat beside her.

"You were crying," Michael said softly. "Are you all right?"

She nodded slowly. "I'm fine."

Monica quickly, almost dismissively, hugged Broken, as women sometimes hug one another for comfort and solidarity. Then she tried to let go, but Broken had wrapped her strong arms around her, burying her head on Monica's shoulder.

Memory was...

If only she could cut it off, like the arm. If only...

[CHAPTER 14]

THE NEWS FROM THE OTHER REFUGEES in the library hadn't been encouraging. All mass transit had been shut down. All flights had been grounded. The Army and the Black Bands had set up checkpoints on all of the roads heading to and from the city.

"I heard a story," one old man whispered in Michael's ear. "I heard that in one of the camps the Army set up, they started to check everyone's ID. Anyone who was a UNP member had to stay in the camp. The rest were let go. And you know what happened next?"

"What?" Michael asked, dreading the answer.

"They started arresting 'em. Some were shot right there."

"Where'd you hear that from?"

The old man was already turning, off to breathe his news in another ear, but not before Michael had glanced up at him. He'd tell that story until the day he died, about the government killing refugees. He would make it a little more dangerous each time, a little more obvious, a little worse.

Then the government would come and arrest him. He'd die in prison not long after. He'd never get to find out whether his story was true or not.

Broken had cheered up considerably, as far as they could tell, and changed Ian on her own. She did a good job.

"We used to help out with babies in the Tower," she muttered by way of explanation.

"You'll have to tell us what it was like to live there, someday," Monica said.

Broken shrugged. Michael studied her, allowing the possibilities to form and swirl all around her. He had tried not to see what lay ahead since the last time, when the thin man had appeared in each...

—*The thin man boarded his light, aerodynamic flyer and laughed. Ian was in his arms.*

—*"I'm just like you," the thin man said to Michael before he shot him.*

—*"I saw this coming. Why didn't you?" said the thin man to Michael before he shot him.*

—*"Shut up!" screamed the thin man; he leveled his gun at Michael's forehead, and pulled the trigger.*

—*The thin man said nothing, and shot Michael.*

He was still there. Michael squeezed his eyes shut, blocking the visions out.

"We need to go," he said. "Now."

Monica looked at him. "Why not stay here?"

"*Trust* me," he seethed. "Let's go."

They trusted him. Broken and Monica picked up what they had, Broken cradling Ian, and followed him out.

They trusted him, but they shouldn't, he thought bitterly. He had no idea what to do next. He hadn't seen anything but his own end at the hands of the thin man, all through the eyes of a Broken who didn't exist yet. There was nothing else.

No move he made could be right. So what should he do?

Keep going, he told himself. Better to keep going. You'll figure something out. For now, just keep moving.

They started walking south, towards New Jersey and the vast spaceport that occupied the Delmarva Peninsula. The weather was frigid, and slowly growing worse. Snow started to fall; first the odd flake, then a few more, and soon a full-blown blizzard.

"We need to find a place to stay for the night," Monica cried, straining to be heard over the howling wind.

"You don't say," growled Michael, more to himself than Monica. She couldn't hear him anyway.

The snow flew fast and thick. Michael leaned into the wind as they struggled to keep moving forward.

"Are we in New Jersey yet?" Broken asked. She was holding Ian inside her coat, pressed to her chest.

"Don't know," Michael said shortly.

"Michael!" Monica called. "I think I see a house up ahead!"

And indeed, a soft yellow light could be seen through the blizzard.

Michael knocked at the door again.

A middle-aged woman opened it a crack. "What do you want?" she asked suspiciously.

"Please, can we come in?" Michael begged.

"Why are you out in this weather?"

"We're refugees," Monica said. "From the city! Please."

The woman scowled. "Only criminals are refugees. The screen said so. You must be some of those UNP people. I'm not sharing my house with terrorists!"

"Wait!" Michael said. "We're not—" But she had already slammed the door in their faces.

"Bet you didn't see that coming, either," Monica sniped. "Now what?"

"I don't see everything. Hey!" He pounded on the door. "Please!"

The woman opened the door a crack. "I've already called the police. Get lost."

They tried the next house, and the next. They were coming back down into a more populated area now, a small town somewhere in New Jersey, but the answer everywhere was the same: Go away. We don't want refugees. We don't want trouble. You're probably criminals if you're running.

"Damn Reformist sons-of-bitches," Monica swore. "This is all their fault, with their stupid propaganda!"

"Didn't you say you really *are* a UNP member?" Michael asked.

"Maybe. Fuck you! You believe this, too?"

"No. But people would be right to be scared of hiding you."

She sighed, and had to agree that this was true.

They huddled against the side of a brick building for warmth. "Why did we leave that library?" Monica complained. "What was the reason? So we could stay out here and die from the cold?"

"We won't die from the cold," Michael said, although in truth he hadn't checked. He was discovering he could block possibilities more effectively by simply keeping his eyes off everyone. He'd been doing that a lot lately.

"Come on," Broken said, standing up. "Snow's bad. There's places to go."

They walked along the backs of the buildings on the main street. Broken tried door handles, one after the other, but nothing opened. Up ahead, a restaurant's lights glimmered invitingly.

"We need to eat," Michael said. "Come on. It'll be warm."

"They might kick us out," Monica pointed out.

Michael reached up into his pant leg and pulled out one of the bills. "We'll be fine. We're paying customers."

Monica stared at him in disbelief. "Why didn't you mention that you had *money* before?"

"I thought I had," Michael said nonchalantly. "Besides, we haven't really needed it yet. Come on, let's go."

"Food," agreed Broken.

"We could have been staying in a *hotel*," Monica seethed. "We could have been eating *well*. I ought to kill you."

◂▸▸ ◂◂▸

Even with a storm raging outside, the restaurant was full. A lot of the people sitting in the booths and at the counter looked like they'd seen better days. There were screens set up all over the place, showing images of the crisis.

"Terrorist actions in the cities of Chicago and Boston have been quelled," intoned an attractive man with perfect hair. He was one of the main newscasters for North America; people trusted him. He wore a tiny white star with black highlights on his lapel—a Reformist pin. That was new. "Other UNP-backed riots and terrorist actions are being contained in Los Angeles and New York. The Peltan Administration says it expects peace to return by the end of the day."

"About time," someone muttered.

"Across the world, the few riots that erupted in Asia and Australia were quickly subdued, and no further terrorist activity has taken place there. Australia is quiet at this hour, as the Peltan Administration prepares for the President himself to address an emergency session of the Senate tomorrow at noon Central Australian Time—ten o'clock tonight for our viewers here. The Administration has issued a warning for any potential terrorists against taking action against government forces."

The scene shifted to a spokesman for the Administration, standing in front of an image of black-clad soldiers fighting. Words on the soldiers' uniforms were barely but obviously visible: "Virtue, Honor, Loyalty, Strength." Others had simply "VHLS" on their helmets. The Reformist credo. The sternly handsome spokesman cleared his throat and spoke. He looked strong and resolute; his brows were knitted together, his jaw jutted out.

"These terrorists pose a threat to our most basic freedoms, and must be stopped. Rest assured that our government will not rest until they all have been killed or captured. Any and all UNP members are encouraged to voluntarily surrender to the government for a loyalty inspection. Most of you are innocent of any wrongdoing, and will be released quickly. However, we *will* find those who are guilty of aiding, abetting and, indeed, *becoming* terrorists. Those who do not comply will be assumed to be on the side of evil."

Someone snorted. His friend shushed him.

"We understand that these are unusual measures. However, we have been elected to protect the security of humanity, and protect it we will. The moral and ethical deterioration of the core membership of the United Nations Party was completed when it rose up against the government it helped to found, and that rotting cancer must be expunged from the body of humanity."

He suddenly took on a softer tone, his eyes relaxing from their intense stare. Now he looked like a sympathetic boyfriend.

"We understand as well that many thousands of innocents and families have been displaced by this terrible crisis. Our hearts go out to them, and to them we say: Your government will be there. Already we have provided hundreds of thousands of tons of food for refugee camps. President Peltan cares about his people, and will see that they are well provided for. Thank you all."

The newsreader reappeared. "In other news, the Emperor of the Rogarians has sent a message communicating his hopes for peace on our world to all humans. The emperor says—"

A surly-looking waitress strode up to them. "Make it quick," she snapped. "You got money, right?"

"Right," Michael said.

"Extra charges today, to cover fees during the crisis." Michael shrugged. Whatever. As long as they were warm and fed, it was worth whatever it cost.. "So what can I get you?"

They ordered. "Hey, can we have a bottle of warm milk for the baby?" Monica asked; Ian was crying, and other customers were starting to shoot glares their way.

"Can't help you. Go next door, if they're still open. Damn broke-ass refugees, they're shutting everything down."

"I'd better go," Monica sighed, scooping up the wailing infant. "I'll be right back."

"Maybe she'll change him," Broken said.

Michael smiled back. "I sure hope so. I can't stand

that stink."

"Good thing he's so important. I'd leave him in the river."

"Got that right," Michael said. "Hey, wait! You're joking? You have a sense of humor?"

Broken shrugged. "Life sucks. So I laugh."

"That's a good way to be, I think," he nodded.

Broken leaned forward. "So. You have a plan? For getting you-know-where?"

Michael shook his head. "I have to level with you. I don't. Besides walking, there's little else for us to do. They're distracted now, but as soon as things die down enough for us to use public transportation again, they'll be back looking for us."

"Tickets have a date?"

He shook his head again. "They're coupons, sort of. We redeem them as soon as we get to, uh, where we're going. Then we can take the next flight, if there's room."

"I want to go to Valen," Broken said wistfully. "I hear it's nice."

"Yeah. Me too. Lots of space, too, but not like here. It's all open and new. All potential, not a decaying ruin."

Broken sighed. "I'd like to have land. I grew up in a tower, spent most of my life there. After that, I lived on the city streets. I want to have somewhere that's just mine, with just me."

This was the most she'd said at once since Michael had met her. He wanted to keep her talking. "Yeah... I'd like that, too. It'd be nice to own a little farm or some-thing. We could go in together. Raise pigs."

Broken wrinkled her nose. "I don't think I like pigs."

"Ever meet one?"

She shook her head. "People say they smell."

"That's not true. Take it from me. Joe owned a little farm, a long time ago, and he had a big fat hog. That old thing just smelled like mud sometimes, not bad at all. Just a normal animal smell."

Broken chewed on that for a while. "Maybe a horse?"

"Horses are a lot of work," Michael said. "We had one for a little while, but we had to sell him."

"Why?"

"Too much money, too expensive. Joe wasn't rich, and he didn't really work. He just sold the eggs from the farm."

"Is he dead?" asked Broken, characteristically blunt.

He nodded. "Yeah. Two years ago, now."

"And you don't have parents?"

"No. They died when I was a kid. I never knew them too well."

"Me, neither," Broken said softly. "The Union took me when I was little, so I don't remember them at all."

Michael didn't know what to say to that. To his surprise, Broken picked up the conversation, changing the subject.

"So do you own the farm now?"

"No," Michael answered. "We had to sell it a few years earlier to pay for his medical bills. So we were in an apartment in Litchfield those last years, which was hard for Joe. He always liked walking around his land."

"I can understand that, I think," Broken said. She looked up at Michael, suddenly intense. "Do you think I really will fly again?"

"Yes," he said, looking away. "It's really possible. If we can do this." It had been true, once. He *had* seen it. What had changed? He peeked at her possibilities one more time.

—The thin man—

—The thin man—

—The thin man—

...

—Broken flew, graceful, beautiful, in the clear, deep blue skies of Valen.

He hadn't seen that in days. His sight was just messing around with him again. "You will," he said. "I'm going to make it happen."

"I believe you," Broken said. And, wonder of wonders, maybe she actually did.

The waitress dropped their food on the table. "Other girl back yet?" she asked.

"No," Michael said. "Soon, probably."

"Here." She slammed a small glass of milk on the table. "That's for the baby. You have a bottle, I hope?"

"Sure," Michael said. "Thanks."

"Stuff it." The waitress, out of breath, dashed to her next customer.

The door banged open, and everyone fell silent. Three Black Bands strode cockily in, toting assault weapons, which they calmly leveled at the diners.

"ID check," one announced. "Get 'em out, people."

"Hey," a reedy man with a thin mustache and a thinner voice said hesitantly, as everyone fumbled for their ID cards, "Can you do this? Is this legal?"

In answer, one of the Black Bands went to stand next to him. "ID card, sir." The other two sniggered.

He showed it to them. They scanned it. A predatory smile spread over the face of the man with the scanner.

"Yeah, he's UNP. Thought so. Come with us, buddy."

"I'm not UNP!" he protested. "I'm not even registered! This is illegal! Come on—" They hauled him from his seat and pushed him out into the snow. An entire squad of Black Bands was in the street, bundling people into a big black hopper.

"Let's go, everyone. Cards out. Sooner we get this done, sooner you can go back to eating."

Timidly, the diners pulled out ID cards. The Black Bands went from person to person, scanning cards. Most they left alone. A few they plucked from their seats, ordering them outside to be packed into the big military-grade hopper, which squatted, waiting, like a menacing black beetle.

"You have one?" Michael asked Broken. She shook her head. "Shit." Michael had a few fakes; he didn't know how good they were. Did any of them have political affiliations? He doubted it.

He found one of the fakes and handed it to a Black Band when he passed by, hand out. The thug scanned it quickly and studied the information. Not finding what he was after, he handed the card back to Michael, and held a hand out to Broken.

"I don't have mine," she said softly.

"My aunt here didn't know she'd need one," Michael tried to explain. "She's not UNP. She doesn't even vote. She's a good citizen, like me. Can you let it slide?"

Instead of responding, he took a needle and jabbed it into Broken's arm, sucking up blood and tissue. She yelped in surprise. He withdrew it and spat its contents into the scanner. It whirred for a second; a record came up.

His eyebrows shot up, and a vicious smile bloomed on his dark features.

"Go wait outside. Both of you. In fact, I'll take you out there myself."

Michael and Broken exchanged startled glances. The Black Band pointed the barrel of his rifle at them. "Get going. Or else I light you up."

"Just go," someone hissed. "They'll set the whole place on fire!"

Michael and Broken stood slowly, covered by the Black Band, and marched outside. Snow was still falling lightly, and the sky was darkening fast.

They couldn't escape. Michael knew it. He only hoped Monica and Ian were safe. Maybe he could get out later... but if they knew who Broken was, it was all lost anyway.

"You see it?" Broken said softly. "See it?"

"What?" Michael was confused.

"*Look.*" she whispered. "How you do."

"No talking!" the Black Band said. "Get in the hopper, *now.*"

She stared imploringly at Michael, and he realized at last what she was talking about. He looked into her possibilities. His vision, for once, didn't mess with him, didn't show him hundreds, thousands of potential scenarios. He saw exactly what she was planning, and nodded sharply.

Without a word, she ducked low and twisted around, leg flashing out. The Black Band toppled to the ground, weapon flying. She pounced on him, screeching a wild berserker war cry, while the others, shouting and cursing, ran to his aid.

She had no chance. There were too many of them.

Michael took his cue and *ran*, not looking back.

He ran like hell, down alleys and side streets, concealing himself wherever he could. Behind him, he could hear weapons fire.

[CHAPTER 15]

BROKEN WHIRLED, FASTER THAN EVEN she had thought possible, and decked the Black Band. He fell like a ton of bricks.

This is fun! she thought, seeing Michael take off. *Good. He saw it.* Nice, having an ally who knew what you were going to do next. She thought about Sky Ranger as she clawed at the face of the Black Band, trying to get to his gun. The others were pounding up behind her. He would have liked Michael, back in the old days. Michael should have been in the Union, a power like that. Why wasn't he?

She spied the gun, and grabbed it. Magnificently, he let go as she ripped it away, turning to face the oncoming throng.

"Yahhhhhhhh!" she shrieked, as loud as she could.

◂▸▸ ◂◂▸

"*Scream. Make a noise. Really, it scares the shit out of them,*" Crimson Cadet said. "*You especially, Sil. You sound like a banshee.*"

She squeezed the trigger. White-hot energy leapt out of the barrel—*Ooo, one of the new plasma rifles! These are from the Rogarians. I like this!*—and crackled through the air, catching one of them in the throat.

The rest aimed and fired, not caring about their comrade on the ground behind her. As the fire seared her, boiled her, burned her, and turned her organs to ash, she thought about the headache she was going to have, and how good it was that she'd already eaten.

Michael ran until he thought his lungs would burst. Night had fallen quickly. Had they even noticed him escape in the chaos? He hid in a copse of trees outside of town for hours, waiting, wanting to leave but desperately needing to stay.

He got his answer when he saw the hulking hopper take off, speeding away toward the city.

Broken, come back to us, he urged silently. They might have loaded her body on board. Did he dare go back into town to check? Had the Black Bands left anyone behind to guard the place?

He had to go. He owed it to Broken to at least check. He needed to find Monica and Ian, too.

You're free, a little voice in his head informed him.

You could keep running, get out of this, live your life.

Michael fought with himself for a moment, then steeled himself and turned back towards the town.

Slowly, furtively, he crept back through the darkness towards the diner. A few lazy streetlights flickered on here and there. It took him more than an hour of careful movements and ducking into alleys and behind bushes whenever someone approached to cover the ground he had run over in just three minutes the last time.

At last, he faced the open lot in front of the diner where the hopper had landed. Two Black Bands swore and laughed on the steps. In the snow, Michael thought he could make out a dark patch, maybe a bloodstain.

No bodies. They'd taken her.

"Michael!" someone hissed in his ear. He jumped, terrified, and whirled to find Monica holding Ian.

"Hey!" he whispered. "Hey, you're all right!"

"Yeah, what happened? They didn't come in the store, so I stayed there. What's going on? Where's B?"

"Took her," Michael said, jerking his chin towards the Black Bands. "Long gone, now."

"What, you didn't save her? Couldn't you see it coming?"

"I can't see everything!" he hissed. "Look, let's get going. She'll catch up if she can."

"How can you say that?" Monica grabbed his arm. "We have to rescue her! They'll *kill* her!"

"They probably already did. I saw a pool of blood out there."

Her face contorted, and she looked about ready to kill *him*. "Don't you *care* at all?"

"Sure, I care, but it's not like it matters. Broken

never *stays* dead."

"What?" said Monica. "You mean that healing thing she does—?"

Michael nodded.

"Well..." she stammered, clearly flustered. "Well— well you're a *jerk* for not telling me before. I was worried sick!"

Michael rolled his eyes. "Let's go. She may be able to catch up."

When Broken opened her eyes, she could barely make out a gunmetal gray ceiling. The floor hummed and rocked beneath her. She had to think about where she was before moving. She remembered the fight, she remembered the *outstanding* plasma gun she'd fired—

Right, she'd died again. They'd put her aboard the hopper. She lay still for a few more agonizing minutes as she healed herself, then attempted to stand up. The world pitched and rolled.

She looked around the cramped cabin she was in. Next to her lay two other bodies, both Black Bands. One was the man she'd been wrestling with. He had holes singed in him, and a surprised expression was still on his face. They'd shot him while trying to take her down, she remembered. He'd been right behind her. She wondered what had been going through his mind when they opened fire.

The other one had most of his throat burned away. She remembered firing that shot. She looked intently at his face. He was just a kid, really. How old had he been when he joined up with the Black Bands? How long had they been around, anyway...? Five, six years, maybe longer. She couldn't remember. She kind of felt sorry for him. Maybe he'd just joined up so he could earn some money. Did he have a sweetheart somewhere, waiting for him?

It didn't matter, really. He was the enemy, and he would have killed her gladly. He was probably another jerk who liked torturing cats.

She still felt a little guilty.

They'd put all the "bodies" together in the hold, without guards. Why would they need any?

She looked around the hold and saw at least twelve plasma rifles. Even better, they were the new ones, the ones she liked.

"Yeeeeah," she murmured happily. Pain still gnawed at her, but it was growing less and less intense. She'd done a lot of healing while unconscious this time. All the better. She needed to be awake for this.

Training for the Union's Law Enforcement Division had been strenuous; Red Knight had tried to teach them everything he could about the business of fighting crime. It was too bad that they hadn't fought much actual crime—they'd been busy tracking down non-registereds and doing the government's dirty work.

She remembered several classes about what to do if you were taken prisoner. Lots of people wanted to kidnap Extrahumans. Broken could sometimes do some things other people couldn't.

She shouldered two of the guns and opened the door to the rest of the hopper. A corridor ran between the hold and the passenger space. Almost at once, an alarm started to blare. Cameras were all over the place; of course they were watching. "Hey!" called a Black Band from the cockpit, struggling up.

She turned and ran towards the back of the hopper, where the emergency exit was. She twisted the release, and the door blew off.

Behind her, the Black Bands were shouting and scrabbling towards her. She looked back once, stuck out her tongue, and jumped.

The night was cold and moonless. She fell, twisting, weightless, rushing toward the gray-black ground far below.

She stretched her arms and felt the wind rushing past. She tilted her head up, and laughed out loud.

It was like flying!

Like *flying*...

The ground rushed up to greet her with a sickening crunch; she blacked out again. Her last thought before impact was *I hope the guns survive.*

She woke up hungry, and in pain worse than she had ever felt before. She had never had to do so much healing so quickly.

She opened her eyes and saw three inky shapes

standing over her. She couldn't make out any features in the dark. She tried to move, but dried blood had frozen her to the ground. "Where'd you come from?" a man with blacked-out teeth demanded. "This your blood? Your guns?"

"Hrrrnnn..." she gasped.

"Saw a Black Band hopper go over not too long ago," said another. "You know about that?"

"UrrriUuuurGhhuuu..." she groaned. "F— f— foooooo...."

"Hungry? We'll feed you. But you have to talk, right?"

"Yuh," she promised. They pulled her free—she only screamed a little—picked her up, and carried her towards a shack nearby.

◄►► ◄◄►

Sky Ranger studied the Black Bands' reports. He liked studying them: It gave him a sense of being in the know.

He paused, reading one.

"Subject killed one CGT"—Civil Guard Trooper— "thought to be KIA in retaliation, massive plasma burns all over body. Subject appeared in AHV"—Armored Hover Vehicle— "5.6 hours later with no apparent injuries. Subject proceeded to remove two weapons from the vehicle, and egressed via the emergency exit. The AHV was flying at 3,500m at the time."

He had known someone, once, who had healed so quickly. And that fake journalist from a few weeks back had wanted to know about...

"Silverwyng?" he whispered. "Could it be?"

He studied the record some more, and found the flight path of the hopper. As soon as he could get free, he'd go look for her. Very strange indeed.

[CHAPTER 16]

MICHAEL AND MONICA SNEAKED OUT of town under the cover of darkness, trying to avoid police, Black Bands, and anyone else who might be feeling nosy. They stuck to back roads and traces of trails, bearing generally south and west as much as they could. Fat, powerful hoppers and light, skinny zippers streaked constantly overhead, searchlights emanating from their metal bellies.

"Think they're looking for us?" Monica whispered.

"Maybe," Michael said. "Or just looking for anybody."

They dodged into a wooded area, and lost themselves between the trees. They could still hear aircraft overhead, but they couldn't really see them anymore. Once, a searchlight passed directly over them, but they held still and were not seen.

"Jesus, help me now," Monica said softly.

Michael stared at her as if she had grown another head.

"What?" she snapped.

"Nothing," he sighed. "Let's keep going."

They trudged on through the snow and the thick undergrowth.

"So, what, you're anti-religious?" Monica said, voice a little shaky.

"No," Michael soothed, trying to make peace. "No, nothing like that. I guess I just didn't figure you..."

"Well, I'm not. Not really. I was a Catholic, when I was a little girl. But that was a long time ago, and I don't really ever go to church, so..."

"...So?"

"So? So what? Who cares. Let's keep going."

They walked in silence for a few more minutes.

"Hey," Michael said. "Look. My, uh, grandfather believed in God. He thought Val Altrera had a connection with God. He was sort of a Valenist, I guess."

"What, that crap about seeing the future? I heard about that. No one can..."

She trailed off. Michael spread his hands wide, grinning sheepishly.

"Yeah," she grumbled, "Well, you're not very *good* at it."

Michael deflated. "I never thought what I can do comes from God, if that matters to you."

"Why should it? Who cares where it comes from?"

"Monica, I'm sorry—"

"Shut up, okay?" She sped up, and he had to struggle to keep up with her. Ian, snug in Michael's pack, started to wail and moan.

"Monica, stop—I need to change him or feed him or something..." He knelt down in the snow and re-moved Ian from the pack. The kid didn't stink; he must be hungry. Michael took a bottle of formula out from inside his coat where he'd been trying to keep it warm, and pressed it to Ian's mouth. He slurped noisily, drib-bling formula on Michael's jacket, pants, and shoes.

"Monica!" he called. No answer.

"She'll come back," he told Ian. "She's just pissed. No, I don't know why, either."

Ian looked up at him, dark eyes wide. Michael ig-nored the rush of possibility, and just held the little boy.

An inescapable sadness washed over him. Didn't mothers always talk about how magical their children were? Was this what they meant?

Ian sucked contentedly on the bottle. The formula sloshed around and drained little by little. The night was cold, but Michael cradled the baby in his arms, keeping him warm.

"For right now," he said to Ian, "You're my son. I'm never ever going to have a son of my own, so I hope it's all right if I borrow you for a while. I'm not going to get another chance..."

Ian finished sucking down the liquid, withdrew his mouth, and spat up all over Michael. All he could do was laugh. Ian joined in.

<>►◄<>

Monica was sitting under a tree, head buried in her arms.

"Hey," he said, approaching.

She raised her head. "Oh. Oh, I thought you'd gone." Her face was streaked with tears. He decided not to say anything this time.

"You want to get going?" he asked, offering a hand.

She ignored it, struggling to her feet on her own. "Yeah. We should find a place to hide out when the sun rises."

"Okay," Michael said. He let her set the pace. They walked in silence for half an hour, ducking under low branches, carving a path through the dense forest. Michael wasn't even sure they were heading south anymore. He'd know when the sun came up.

He thought about what he'd learned about living in the woods. Joe had taught him how to make a fire; that sounded good about now, but fires would be easy to see from the air. Worse, he didn't have any of the materials he'd need, like tinder. Joe had also showed him how to pitch a tent. They didn't have tents, either. Michael wished Joe had taught him how to navigate by the stars. But maybe Joe hadn't known. Or maybe he hadn't wanted to tell. Joe died with a lot of secrets.

Like where he'd got his power from. Michael had actually asked once, when he was ten.

Don't know, was all Joe had said. But it seemed like a lie to Michael. It could be true, he supposed... but probably not. Joe had been too smart a man to leave it at "don't know."

It developed early in Michael. He'd cried for hours

while Joe patiently tried to explain.

"Grampa, I saw a lady dying! In the mirror!" Michael screamed. He was six.

Joe gave Michael a hug. "Wasn't real," he said. "Just a possibility."

Michael trembled. "It could happen?"

Joe nodded. "There are lots of possibilities. And you and me, we sometimes see some of them. Does that make sense?"

Michael thought. "No!" he said. "Why doesn't anybody else see it, too?"

"Because we're special," Joe replied. "And we are. You are. I am. This is something only we and a few others know how to do."

Michael looked at Joe and was suddenly flooded with possibilities. "Joe..." he said. "You're going to die!"

"Not now," Joe said soothingly. "Not yet. But everybody dies. You're seeing some of it."

"I wish I wasn't," Michael cried bitterly. "I don't want to see."

"Me either," Joe said softly. "But we do. You and me. So there it is."

Michael stopped crying. "There it is," he repeated sadly. Joe hugged him again.

Joe was there when the terrible dreams came. He understood them. Joe was there when Michael looked in the mirror and threw up because of what he saw. Joe was there when Michael saw, for the first time, his own death.

<>► ◄<>

"A thin man," Michael kept saying, over and over. "A thin man killed me."

"He hasn't killed you yet," Joe said. "And you may be able to get out of it. Remember, these are not things that definitely will happen. They're just possibilities."

"So I may not die like that?"

"No. In fact, you probably won't."

"There it is?" Michael whispered.

Joe smiled. "There it is."

<>► ◄<>

After Joe's death, Michael had grown up very quickly. He still missed him terribly. What would he have said right now, Michael wondered. What would Joe have done?

He'd probably tell me to stop being so sentimental, and get on with it, Michael thought wryly. He marched ahead, listening to Ian's breathing as the baby fell asleep. One foot in front of the other, now. One, two. One, two. Keep up the pace.

"Michael?" Monica said, surprising him.

"Yeah?"

"Are we going to die today?"

He took a quick peek. "You really want to know?" he asked.

"Yes. Please, tell me."

"Possibly. But it's hard for me to tell one day from another."

"Oh." She lapsed back into silence for a while.

Then, "Michael?"

"Yeah?"

"Do you think Jane and Lydia and Andrew and Shawn and Fred are in heaven? I mean, can you see any of that?"

He tried to absorb the question. "Uh. I don't really know. I never see that..." He glanced over at her. Possibilities swirled... but here and now, Monica had a hungry, needful look on her face, like a drowning man wishing for a lifeboat.

"If there is such a place, they're in it," Michael said. "I can't believe they're suffering, wherever they are." It was lame. But maybe it would be enough.

She sighed. "Yeah." Her face started to harden again.

"They're probably with God," Michael said quickly. "They probably got to meet him face to face."

Monica surprised him by giggling. "I bet Andrew is really surprised. Rätons don't believe in an afterlife, and Andrew thinks like a Räton. So if he's having one, he's pretty surprised right now."

"You're probably right."

"And Lydia is bossing God around. I bet he can't do anything without her saying so. She was always so bossy..." Her voice caught. Michael quickly took up the slack.

"How about Jane?" he asked. "I bet she's really happy, finally."

"She was always so sad..." Monica said. "At least all of her children—our children—escaped. I guess it was a blessing that they were taken away."

"Yeah." He found himself with nothing else to add.

Silence returned, this time to stay until dawn.

◆►◄◆

Broken ate like a horse. The men gathered around her watching, open-mouthed, as she inhaled a vast pile of potatoes, a bowl of unspecified vegetables, a bit of chicken, a gallon of milk, half a block of cheese, and most of a loaf of bread.

When she was done, she let off an enormous belch. The men applauded.

"Damn," said the guy who had first spoken to her, "You're an eater."

"I was hungry," she said. "Sorry."

"No trouble. I guess there's no more for us, though, right, boys?" They laughed. "Okay, but serious time. You gonna answer questions like you said?"

"Yah," she agreed.

"Okay. Now. What were you doing out there?"

"Jumped out of a hopper."

They exchanged glances. "Don't lie."

"It's true," she said.

"And you're okay? That makes no sense."

"... Parachute?" she tried.

"Where is it, then?" another man asked.

She shrugged. "Don't know. Fell off."

"Hang on." A new man, who had a jarring combination of dark skin and radioactive green hair, entered. "What kind of hopper?"

"Black Bands," she said. "But I got away."

The green-haired man leaned closer. "How do you know we won't turn you in? Huh?"

"You don't seem like Black Bands," she said simply. And it was true. They didn't. She'd been around long enough to know who generally fell on which side. These guys weren't going to be wearing black armbands with VHLS initialed on them any time soon. It wasn't that they seemed disorganized and purposeless—though that was true. They just had a certain look in their eyes. They looked *hunted*.

They moved off and talked in hushed tones for a minute. She caught some of the conversation. "Banders... come back... flight path... next house..." They all looked at her and came to some sort of decision.

"Okay, we're going to go on to the next place. You can come with us, but we got to scan you first."

"Scan away," she said. "I'm not carrying anything."

They scanned her with three separate instruments, and found nothing.

"All right. Come on."

"Hey," she said, regretting it almost as soon as she opened her mouth. "How do you know *I'm* not one of them?"

They laughed again. "You're not the type," said Green Hair. "You just some crazy lady. You can't be one of them and look like you do."

Fair enough. She did look pretty bad, she was sure. Her clothes were caked in blood, her silver hair was matted and unkempt, and her face... was her face. She was used to it. She rose and followed the men outside.

There were six men in this outfit, whatever it was.

They had taken her guns from her, which she figured was fine since they weren't hers to begin with, and added them to a big stash in a mag-van parked in a dirt driveway.

"Okay," said Green Hair, who seemed to be the leader. "Everybody get in. We goin' now." Green Hair's English was a little strange, almost lilting; he sounded like he might be from the Caribbean, or maybe South America. The men piled into the mag-van, which started up with a deafening roar. The ground engine was an old internal combustion relic. She wondered what they were using for fuel. It sure stank, whatever it was.

Broken sat on one of the seats next to two leering, mostly drunk men. "Hey, gran'ma," one slurred. "Taking a ride?" His companion found this hilarious and giggled wildly.

"Not your grandma," she snorted. Her hair fooled a lot of people into thinking she was older.

"You look like you been through hell," a more sober man said, squinting through the darkness. "That blood on there?"

"Yuh," she assented.

"Yours?"

"Most. Some belongs to a Black Band, I think."

The men clapped and shouted, obviously disbelieving.

She smiled back. She didn't care what they thought of her; she knew what she'd done.

The van strained and groaned, then rolled forward on heavily treaded tires.

"Keep off the main roads," Green Hair said. "Can't hit a checkpoint."

"Yeah, yeah," said the driver, a grizzled white man in his sixties. "We'll be fine."

The van bumped and jostled down the driveway. "Turn on the headlights," Green Hair said mildly.

"Oh, right," the old man said, and pulled a switch. The road ahead was illuminated—badly. One light must be out, Broken reasoned.

The main road was about half a mile down the dirt driveway, after which Broken, still full of food, was starting to feel a little sick.

"Where is it?" the old man asked.

Green Hair sighed loudly. "Turn left." As they nudged onto the main road, the county magnetics took over, and the van lurched a few feet off the ground. Broken could hear the wheels retracting with a horrible screech and a scrape, and then there was nothing but the quiet hum of the electromagnetic generator. The van hesitantly powered forward and picked up speed.

"Keep going on this road, then go right at the old post," Green Hair said. "You know the one."

"Yeah, yeah," the old man grumbled.

The van sped soundlessly through the New Jersey night. Broken forced her dinner back down (she remembered now, she always got carsick) and tried to focus on not throwing up.

I hope Michael is doing better, she thought. To her right, the first rays of dawn were beginning to appear.

[CHAPTER 17]

To Michael's consternation, the sun rose directly in front of them. They were heading southeast—back towards the river.

"We need to head the other way," he said. Monica groaned.

"You can see the future, but you can't even tell which direction we're going in?" She was teasing. Mostly.

He shrugged gamely. "I don't do directions." She snorted, half-smiling. Ian started to make a fuss, and Michael smelled something foul. "Can you change him?" he asked. "I did it the last three times."

"He doesn't like me," Monica said, looking at Ian. "He gets it—" she swallowed hard, "He gets it all over me."

Michael laughed. "He does that to everyone."

Ian was now starting to really get going. He howled and screamed, as if someone was sticking him with pins.

"I'll do it," Michael volunteered at last. He didn't want to drive Monica away again.

"Oh, I'll help," Monica said huffily. "Damn it! He is *loud*." Michael rummaged through his pack for diapers while Monica fought with Ian's diaper.

"Hey, Michael?" she asked.

"Yeah?" he said, withdrawing a new plastic poop catcher. He hated these things.

"When... when you look at me, what do you see?"

He glanced up at her, startled by the question. She had that old lopsided smile on her face; he hadn't seen it in too long.

"Maybe you can tell my fortune," she said, green eyes mischievous.

"Um, well," he stammered, and met her gaze.

—*Monica walked alone, across a desert. She carried a baby. It wasn't Ian.*

—*There was a room, in the city on faraway Calvasna, where she waited for her husband to come home. When he did, she was overjoyed, but afraid at the same time. Did the man look familiar? Michael almost recognized him.*

—*There was a green field, and Monica, dressed in blue, hiked through it towards a huge ramshackle house. Two people flew above it in graceful, sweeping arcs.*

—*Monica sat in a blooming garden, surrounded by her grandchildren.*

—*She waited in a cell. She'd be there for the rest of her short life.*

"There's a lot of possibilities," he said. "But one...

I saw you in a meadow, walking towards a big house. I think your friends were there. And another... I saw you married."

"To who?"

"No idea."

She smiled crookedly. "It's good... to think I have a future, no matter what it might be. At least we won't be here forever."

Snap. Click.

Their heads shot up at the sudden sound. Michael started as he found himself looking down the barrel of an old-fashioned machine gun.

"Stand up," commanded the machine gun's owner. "Slowly."

Four men, each holding an identical machine gun, gestured at them. Their faces were covered; they wore camouflage from head to toe. Where had they come from? "Let's go. Nice and easy."

Michael and Monica stood up. Ian, almost as if he realized the danger, had become eerily quiet.

"Hands high," one said, gesturing. They held their hands in the air, palms open. "All right. Put 'em behind your head. You're prisoners."

Michael's mouth was dry. He'd seen these guys in a few visions, but he hadn't really expected them, at least not just yet. He'd been hoping not to see them at all.

"Hey, what are we prisoners for?" Monica demanded. "Who are you guys?"

Two of them trained their weapons on her, impassive behind camouflage bandannas. She shut up.

A vivid memory struck Michael. He had been nine years old, and he had looked in the mirror one morning.

—A man in camouflage just like these men had a gun pressed to his head. "Start over, traitor! Start all over again!" Michael started again, but the first word came out all wrong. The man in camouflage shot him in the head.

"Follow me," the leader said. "We have you covered from behind. Try anything, we shoot you." He seemed very matter-of-fact about it. Michael believed him. The leader marched off into the forest.

"The baby?" Michael hesitantly asked, looking back. But one of the men had grabbed the pack, baby and all. Ian mewled, confused, frightened, and diaper still full of shit.

The woods opened into a clearing, in which stood a rundown cabin. A trail of smoke curled out of a slender stovepipe. Michael could smell the pleasant tang of wood burning.

The four men tramped up to the door, keeping their muzzles trained on Monica and Michael. The leader went inside for a second, then reemerged.

"Inside," he barked. They obeyed, stepping onto the wood porch and through the heavy oak door into a darkened room where an old wood stove sat, radiating warmth. Two men sat behind a table, reading what looked like newspapers. Behind them hung a familiar yet shocking sight: a flag with thirteen red-and-white stripes, and a blue, star-filled canton. The old flag of the

United States, banned since the end of the Last War. They'd seen it only in textbooks and movies about the war, for the most part—

> Joe held the old piece of cloth reverently. "We worshiped it when I was a boy. I took up a gun to try and defend it. Can you believe that? But I saw the end coming." He tapped his head. "So I deserted my post. I took this with me, though. It used to stand for something a lot better than what it ended up standing for." He sighed. "But they don't tell you that. To the Australians"—Joe always referred to the Confederation government as "the Australians"—"it's just a symbol of evil, of the wickedness of Greenleaf's administration. My own dad hated Greenleaf. But he loved this. It's hard to say why, really, but they were two separate things to him."
>
> He put the old flag away. "I suppose it is just a thing, and that's that."

—but every once in a while... they'd seen it somewhere else. Like most people of their generation, Michael and Monica had never seen anyone display one freely. So they did what Americans their age did when they saw that old flag; they gaped, and a little shiver ran up and down their spines.

One of the men saw where their gaze lay. He grunted. "Calls to something in the blood, don't it. I know the feeling."

"That flag's illegal," Monica declared flatly. The men laughed a short, mirthless laugh.

"Yeah, so it is. So are we. So are you, most likely. UNP?"

Monica flushed. "I am," she said defiantly.

"Thought so. Why else wander around the woods, lost, in the cold, with a baby crying so loud the dead will come back to life? How 'bout you?" The man behind the table pointed at Michael.

"They want me for other reasons," Michael said.

The man nodded. "Fair enough, right? I'm Colonel Wayne." He extended a hand. Michael took it gingerly; the man had a grip like iron. He did not offer his hand to Monica. "This is the 1st New Jersey Regiment of the American Liberation Army." The men surrounding them nodded, still keeping a hand on their weapons. "You are our prisoners, I'm afraid."

"Why are we prisoners?" Monica wanted to know. Colonel Wayne kept looking at Michael, ignoring her.

"You were trespassing on our woods," Wayne said. "These are dangerous times. We can't trust anyone. You've been scanned; you were as soon as you came in here. We're pretty satisfied you're not wearing a transmitter or any other signal device, but we can't be sure, right? You might be spies. *Lots* of spies around." He jutted his chin out. "We *kill* spies."

Colonel Wayne, Michael realized, studying his face, was at most twenty years old.

—*Black Bands opened fire; he fell, guts torn out. He made a few motions, trying to put his intestines back in, then collapsed and mercifully blacked out.*
—*He ran right at the company of soldiers in front of the vast, pillared ConFedMil building, screaming his head off. His leg still hurt. He yelled out someone's name, and fell in a hail of bullets and plasma fire.*

—The hopper was over the city. "Drop it!" Wayne yelled. But something was wrong. Fire erupted everywhere.

Possibilities. Michael looked away, aware of a growing throbbing behind his temples. Violence was this young man's destiny. He'd have a deeper look later.

Three short, sharp shots rang out, and echoed in the air. Michael and Monica jumped. Wayne laughed.

"That's just Kent hunting out there. Probably shot a squirrel." He grinned at his men. "Dinner!"

He suddenly scowled at them again. "Search them. Thoroughly. Go easy on the woman, but make sure she ain't hiding anything. Right?"

"Right," said one of the "soldiers." He still wore his camouflage bandanna. Michael wondered if he was wearing a leer behind it.

Scanners and other equipment were brought out, and they were patted down, too. They found the money and the tickets.

"Trying to get off planet, huh?" Wayne asked. "That's the coward's way out, my friend." Michael didn't say a word.

"Those are ours," Monica protested.

"You think I'm a *thief?*" Wayne said icily. All movement suddenly came to a halt.

Kid or no, Michael realized, he was dangerous. He stood and advanced on Monica in two massive strides. He stood nearly twice as tall as she did. He glared down at her. "Are you questioning my *honor*, woman?"

"Wayne," one of the camouflaged men said warningly.

"Shut up, Parker! *Answer* me, *woman*. Did you or did you not imply that I was a thief?"

"I—I was just saying—it looked like you were going to take it, like the Black Bands did—"

He reared back and slapped her. She staggered across the room.

"Hey!" Michael cried, rushing forward.

A big hand clamped down on his shoulder. Parker, the soldier who had tried to calm Wayne down, shook his head at him. "Better not, kid," Parker said quietly. Michael gratefully allowed himself to be restrained.

"Don't *ever* question my honor!" Wayne spat. "I don't want your *shit*. We're *Americans*, we don't *steal*. And we are *not* like the Black Bands!"

Monica, clutching her cheek, stared at Wayne, stunned. She glanced over at Michael quickly, then looked away again.

"Um," said a soldier. "They're clean, as far as I can tell."

"Here," Wayne said, tossing the money and the tickets back towards Michael. They landed on the floor. "Pick 'em up."

Michael did as he was told.

"Now get them imprisoned somewhere," Wayne said. "I don't care where."

"Uh, Wayne?" a soldier said. Wayne shot him a death glare. "*Colonel*. We have no space for 'em."

"Then they can use *your* room, Banner," Wayne snapped. "Get going."

Banner prodded Michael in the back with the butt of his rifle. "You heard him. Get going." Out of the corner of his eye, he saw someone help Monica to her feet.

They were led down a flight of stairs into what Michael assumed would be a rather rustic basement. To his surprise, it was a fully furnished suite of rooms, possibly larger in area than the house above. "Here," said the soldier, the one Wayne called Banner, opening a door into a small room with a cot and some clothes scattered here and there. "I guess you'll have to share."

"Sorry about your room," Michael said. "Uh. Banner."

—The guns silenced him.
—An armored hovercraft leveled and fired. The shell took his head off.
—He bled to death in a desert, with only the unrelenting sunlight as a companion.

Were they all like this? Michael looked away.

"No big thing," Banner shrugged. He pulled off his bandanna and shoved it into a duffel bag, then he crammed the rest of his things inside.

"You got a rank, too?" Michael asked.

"Nah. Only Wayne gets a rank." Banner was a large guy—they were all large—with blond hair and an incredibly thick neck. His head looked kind of like a potato, Michael thought.

—"Mom!" he cried, feeling his chest. Holes, everywhere. "Mommy! Mommy!" Redness crept into his field of vision. Was someone standing over him? Darkness.
—The hopper was over the city. "Drop it!" Wayne yelled. Banner flinched. He suddenly realized he hadn't put the safety on. Fire erupted everywhere.

Michael sighed. These days, he only ever seemed to see people's untimely ends. Why couldn't he see something ordinary, like someone going for a walk or taking a leak? "Well. Thanks, Banner. Where's the bathroom?"

"Uh. Knock on the door if you need to go or change or something."

"We had a baby with us," Michael reminded him.

"Oh. Um. I don't know what's happening with that. I'll go check. I got to lock you in. So go on in." He gestured. Michael went inside and sat on the cot next to Monica. Banner shut and locked the door.

Tears were streaming down Monica's face. She put her fist in her mouth and curled up on the cot.

"Hey, you okay?" He touched her shoulder. She whirled and slapped his hand away.

"Fuck you," she whimpered.

"Does it hurt? Let me see," he said.

"*Go away.*" She turned away from him, and wouldn't say another word, though she sniffled from time to time. He settled on to the floor and fell asleep.

When he woke up, he realized that Ian was still missing. He scrambled to his feet. Monica had passed out on the bed, and was snoring softly. "Hey!" he called softly. "Anyone out there?"

The door opened a crack. Banner poked his head in. "What?"

"The baby," Michael said. "Remember?"

"Uh? Oh! Yeah, Wayne wanted to play with him. Probably still upstairs."

Wayne wanted to *play* with Ian? Huh. "Are we going to get him back?"

"Oh, yeah, sure," Banner said distractedly. "He'll be back down."

"Okay, then," Michael said. "Uh. Thanks."

"Sure thing," Banner said. He shut the door. Michael sat back down on the floor, and tried to imagine Wayne playing with a baby. With *his* baby.

[CHAPTER 18]

TIME CRAWLED. EVERY ONCE IN A WHILE, Michael would hear boots clump across the boards above his head, and sometimes he heard voices and shouts. Monica slept soundly, showing no signs of waking any time soon. He spent the day lost in thought.

An American "liberation army"... he pondered that for a while. These guys were just a bunch of kids trying to resurrect a country everyone said was better left dead and gone. Humanity had been united as a single nation for over fifty years. Who were they kidding? Maybe they just liked shooting at things and living in the woods. At least it was mostly peaceful.

Where was Broken? Had she escaped? What would they do to her if she hadn't? Would they take her back to the Extrahuman Union? Would she tell Sky Ranger everything? He fervently hoped she was okay, and that she was still free.

When it came to Sky Ranger and the Union he couldn't be sure, even now, where her loyalties ultimately lay.

Monica... He took a moment to look at her sleeping form. She'd been through too much in the past couple of days. She'd lost her home and family, and had her political beliefs outlawed. Now she was stuck in the woods, caught by a group of possibly-addled young men.

She was what, nineteen? Twenty? She sighed in her sleep. She had lovely hair, Michael caught himself thinking. He banished the thought quickly.

He hoped her dreams were peaceful.

A knock on the door. "Food comin' in," Banner said. "Step back from the door. There's three of us."

"I'm back," Michael called. The door opened and Banner stuck his head in. He grinned and shoved two plates of food into the room. "Hey, Banner," Michael said. "Where's that baby we had?"

"Colonel Wayne, last I saw," said Banner. "Hey, we got some news. President made a speech. It's martial law, the Senate has been disbanded. All the UNP Senators got arrested."

"I don't care," Michael said.

Banner fixed him with an intense stare. "Guy's a dictator."

"I knew that."

Banner looked crestfallen. "Okay. Just thought you'd want to know." He withdrew, and locked the door again.

"Hey!" Michael yelled after him, feeling crazy and impulsive. "You're going to die in fire, you know! You're

going to yell for your *mom!*" Banner, perhaps fortunately, didn't return. Michael seethed.

Monica stirred. "Way to piss off the enemy," she
said. "He was nice."

"Oh, you're up?" Michael said irritably. "Well, if
you hadn't noticed, he's keeping us prisoner."

"What crawled up your ass?" Monica grabbed
her plate and started eating. Michael huffed and paced
around the room for a few minutes before picking up his
own plate and eating fitfully. The meat was tough and
stringy, and it tasted funny. He tried not to think about
what it might have been.

"Hey, sorry I was mean to you before," Monica
said. "Really. It's just been a hard couple of days."

"Good for you," Michael snarled. "Other people
have had it rough, too. Not that you notice. All about
you! And do you ever stop complaining? Could have
been you in that fire, too, if not for me! And what thanks
do I get, but you bitching and complaining all the fucking
time!" He whirled away from her, panting angrily. He felt
oddly empty, and glanced back at her.

Monica looked like she'd been struck again. She
even rubbed her cheek, which was still red. "Hey," she
began, eyes big, tears forming. "Hey, I didn't—"

"Oh, stuff it," he snapped bitterly. Monica started
to cry.

He listened to her sniffle for a few minutes, until
he couldn't stand it anymore. "Stop crying," he said.
"Stop. Come on."

"Fuck you," she said, miserable.

He sat on the ground, still fuming.

"They have Ian," he pointed out. "Did you even notice he was gone? You can't even be bothered to change his diaper. But they have him, that Wayne guy has him. I don't know where he is."

"Oh." Monica got herself under control after a few minutes. "Okay. What do we do?"

"We're in prison!" he exploded. "We can't do *anything!*"

"You're a prophet!" she yelled, standing, "Can't you *see* something for us to do?"

"No, I fucking can't!" he screamed back, right in her face.

"Well, why not?" she demanded, crossing her arms over her chest. "Some prophet!"

His shoulders slumped. "It doesn't work that way, I told you. I can't do a damn thing. I only get flashes… and they aren't always useful." He looked up into her eyes.

—Monica kissed him. "I love you," she said. He was so happy.

What the hell? What had he just seen? He dismissed it, looking away.

"You're no help," she said.

"I try." He wasn't angry anymore, but he couldn't bring himself to apologize to her.

Did he really see what he thought he had seen? He couldn't picture himself even *liking* Monica right now.

They sat in opposite corners of the room, she on the cot, he on the floor, for many long minutes until a knock came at the door.

"Stan' back," Banner said. "Comin' in."

"Back," Michael called wearily.

Banner and Parker entered, toting their weapons. Another soldier followed, carrying Ian.

"Ian!" Michael and Monica said at the same time, springing to their feet.

The other soldier handed Ian to Monica, and pointed at Michael. "You. Come upstairs."

"Okay," Michael said, glancing back at Monica. She looked away.

What? Not even a final "fuck you" for good luck? he thought perversely. The door closed behind him, and they led him upstairs.

Colonel Wayne was sitting at his table again, this time alone. Some of the other soldiers were hanging around, watching with interest.

"We heard you two yelling at each other," Wayne said.

Shit, thought Michael. *Now what?*

"So," Wayne said. "You can see the future?" His eyes gleamed with greed and ambition. "Is that true? We heard you two fighting about it down there."

Shit, shit, shit, Michael thought, panicking. Of all the people to actually *believe* it... What would they do to him? He glanced around at their possibilities, but saw nothing of any use. They just died, over and over again.

Wayne's expression soured. "Talk, kid," he said. "Or else." All around him, weapons powered on with a shrill whine.

Shitshitshitshit—!

Michael's brain was scrabbling around so frantically for a plausible lie that he accidentally spat out the truth. "Yes."

Well, that's it. Good work, idiot.

Wayne leaned forward. "You a, uh, Extrahuman? One of those?"

"I guess," Michael said nervously.

"Extrahumans are slaves," Joe had said. "We're just people with gifts. Don't ever say you're one of them."

But there was nothing else to say.

"So you see the future, huh?" Wayne was saying. "Can you see what's going to happen, say, tomorrow?"

Parker snorted. He didn't seem to buy any of it. Wayne shot him a dirty look, then turned back to Michael.

"Well, kid? Can you tell me what's going to happen tomorrow?"

"It—it doesn't work that way," Michael said. He seemed to be saying that a lot. "I, uh, can only see what's going to happen to individuals. And I have to be looking at them. It, uh, comes in flashes. Little bits and pieces. I don't see everything. I don't control what I see." He laughed nervously. "It's really useless! I couldn't see this coming, could I?"

"So you never saw us coming at all?" Wayne said, frowning.

"I knew you were a possibility," Michael said. "But that's all I see, just possibilities. What I see might not happen, it's just, um, possible."

"I see," Wayne said.

"Useless, right?" Michael said. He could feel himself shaking.

"So," Wayne said, licking his lips, "What 'possibilities' do you see for me?" He spread out his arms. "What's going to happen to me?"

Michael looked directly into the young man's deep green eyes.

—Wayne leveled his gun at the oncoming government soldiers—

"I see you fighting. It looks like a desert—"

—But the soldiers fired first. Wayne fell, cursing them. They ran up to him to finish him off. "Son of a bitch," said one before he blew Wayne's head off.

Michael hesitated.

"And?" Wayne said.

"Um. They killed you. Government troops. One called you a son of a bitch." Wayne looked unimpressed. "Sorry, that's all I'm—"

—There was a room full of men. It was this room, but at night, and full. Wayne was speaking. "We need to go to Australia, right now! If we wait, it'll be too late!"

"You're insane," said a lean black man. "I'm not going."

"Then stay, coward!" Wayne yelled, jumping onto the table. "I'm going to fight for freedom." Dead silence followed. Someone snickered.

"Oh," Michael said.

"What?"

"You were trying to get a bunch of men to go to Australia. One of them wasn't listening to you."

Wayne focused his intense gaze on Michael again. "Where were we?" he asked. Everyone in the room held his breath.

"Right here," said Michael. "In this room."

"A fucking spy," Parker said.

"No way," Banner said. "We didn't even know it was gonna happen here 'til just an hour ago."

"Shut up!" snapped Wayne. "You see that in your head?" he asked Michael.

"Yes," Michael said.

Wayne sat back and nodded. "Just so happens that there's going to be a big gathering of all the resistance groups in the area here tomorrow. We're going to be talking about that very subject."

"I suggest you listen to them, then," Michael said. "Because I see nothing but death for all of you if you go to Australia."

"Maybe you'll come *with* us," Wayne said, grinning nastily. "'Cause we're going anyway." The men shifted uneasily. Wayne glared at them, and they stood still again.

Michael swallowed hard. *Me and my big mouth.*

Wayne kept Michael near him for the rest of the day, and forced him to describe, in graphic detail, how each man in the room might die. The room emptied out quickly.

"So, you Union?" asked Wayne at one point. Michael shook his head. "That's illegal, you know. All the animals oughta be in the zoo, right?"

Michael fought down his anger. This man was the type to use him for target practice without a moment's hesitation. "It's illegal to own your own weapons, too, isn't it?"

"Who says we own these?" Wayne said, grinning wickedly. "They don't belong to us. They're the Confederation's!" He cackled madly.

Figures. Michael looked away, saying nothing.

"Hey, that woman downstairs, she your girlfriend?" Wayne asked, leering at him.

"No," Michael said shortly. "She's not."

"Baby hers? Or yours?"

"Neither. Belonged to someone who died."

"Uh-huh." Wayne obviously didn't care about that. "You got a girl, then, kid?"

"No."

"A boy, then? You a pigsticker?" Wayne laughed again.

Pigsticker? "No," Michael said. "I don't. And I'm not."

"So what are you running from, Mike? Confeds want you?"

"Something like that."

"Can't think it's about not being in the Union. Reformists don't like the Union. Did you know that, Mike?"

"Yes."

"Ain't it the truth. Mike, you ever say the Pledge of Allegiance?" Michael shook his head. Wayne sprang out of his chair and stood ramrod straight, hand over his heart, facing the forbidden flag. "Well, this is the way it goes. 'I pledge allegiance to the President of the United States of America, and to the flag of the republic for which it stands. May God Bless America.' Now you say it."

Michael stood, faced the flag, placed his hand over his heart and stumbled through the pledge, garbling the words as he went. Wayne yelled at him. "You can't get it! You can't get it! What kind of American are you! Now say it *again*, 'til you get it *right!*"

So Michael did, trembling, repeating the words while Wayne trained his rifle on him. He made it through with no mistakes the second time.

"Good going," Wayne said, satisfied. He sat down. "Now say it twenty times, so you *really* know it by heart. It's a sacred oath."

Michael said the words over again, and messed up on the third run through. Wayne sprang out of chair again and pressed the muzzle of his gun against Michael's temple. "Start over, traitor!" he hissed. His breath reeked of beer. "Start all over again!"

Michael's heart skipped a beat.

Not here. Not now. Not now... Michael gathered his memory together and exhaled. He could see the words of the pledge in his mind.

Michael slowly recited the pledge again, then again, then again and again, flawlessly each time.

"Good," Wayne said after the twentieth repetition. "Not too bad. But you fucked up, so I'm gonna have to ask you to stand right there. Don't move." He trained the gun on him. "Don't move a damn inch."

[CHAPTER 19]

WAYNE LET HIM GO BACK DOWNSTAIRS as night began to fall. "Hey, remember, you need to be up early tomorrow for the big meeting, so no staying up too late," he said jovially, as he shoved Michael into the small room with Monica. "You two have a nice night together, though!" They could hear him cackling as he clattered back up the stairs.

Monica's eyes went wide when she saw Michael. "Oh, God, are you all right?" She cupped his face in her hands. "What happened? He didn't hit you, did he?"

"I'm okay," Michael said. "I think." He collapsed on the cot, which Monica quickly vacated. "He didn't hit me. He almost shot me."

To the surprise of both of them, he started to cry, tears running down his cheeks as hard sobs racked his body.

"Michael?" Monica said, panicking. "Michael, what happened? Michael!"

"I—I saw him shoot me once, when I was nine," Michael gasped. "I saw a moment. I just lived through it. I don't know how. If I had missed one word—I *saw* it. I *saw it.*" Tears rolled down his cheeks. "God, I don't want to die."

"It's okay, you're still alive," Monica said softly. "You're still here." He found himself in her embrace. They clung to each other like that, Monica holding him and rocking back and forth with him, until Ian woke up and demanded attention.

They listened to the sounds of Wayne and his pals drinking and laughing above them that night. Ian wailed constantly.

"Hey," Monica wondered. "You think he's teething?"

"Could be. He need a diaper change?"

"Yeah. Can you get Banner?"

Michael pounded on the door. No one answered. "Great. He's probably upstairs partying," he said.

Monica shook her head. "Some 'army' this is. They better hope they never face a real one."

"They will," Michael said grimly. "Confeds and Black Bands."

"You saw?" He nodded. "When?"

"Don't know. But soon, probably. They all get killed."

"Oh." She was silent for a moment. "That's too bad. I kind of liked Banner."

"Yeah, he's not so bad," Michael said. "But Wayne... I don't think the world will miss him much."

"Yeah," Monica growled, a spark of anger igniting in her. "Son of a bitch."

Ian cried louder. For a moment, Michael envied him; they were all hungry and tired, but Ian was the only one who could freely express it. He and Monica had to try to hold together, to control what little they could.

"Hey," Michael said. "Sorry about earlier. I was just frustrated. I shouldn't have taken it out on you."

"It's okay," she said, not meeting his eyes. "It happens."

It occurred to Michael that he barely knew Monica at all. He'd fix that, if they ever got out of here.

Finally, the party upstairs ebbed, and Banner thundered down to the basement. He opened the door.

"Oh!" he said. "Damn, I forgot. Uh. You two want food? Pee?"

"Both would be nice," Michael said. "She can go first."

"I'll take Ian," she said, hoisting him onto her shoulder.

"Hey," Banner said softly. "Sorry about Wayne. He's a good guy, really. He just gets a little nuts every now and then."

"Every now and then...? Come on," Monica snarled. "You're all crazy all the time!" Banner looked down, dejected.

"Hey, I believe you," Michael said quickly. "We all go

a little crazy sometimes. I bet you do too, right, Banner?"

Banner nodded. "Banner isn't my real name. When we joined up, we all had to take the names of heroes from American history. My real name is Steve."

"Good to know ya, Steve," Michael said. They nodded at one another warily.

"Come on, miss," Banner said to Monica. "You know where it is."

The next morning, Wayne woke Michael up early so he could be in the room when everyone came in to the conference. "Can you tell me if they're going to want to go to Australia?" he asked Michael. "If they'll vote yes or no?"

"I'll try," Michael said. "I don't guarantee anything. All I see are possibilities."

"Don't fuck up," Wayne warned.

Michael took up his station on the far side of the room, opposite the door. He heard the roar of combustion engines outside. The first of the "delegates" had arrived.

The first to enter were two graying, withered men who wore old uniforms from the *real* U.S. Army, which had been disbanded after the Last War. They had a hard, cruel look about them. Wayne sprang to his feet when they entered.

"Sarge, good to see you," he said to the shorter one, the leader. "How you doing?"

The man scowled at Wayne. "Hello, Anderson. That uniform isn't regulation."

"Sorry, Sarge," Wayne said, with a grin and a shrug. "Regulation uniforms are hard to find these days."

Sarge nodded and sat with his compatriot far away from Wayne, conversing in low tones.

Michael barely needed to use his talent. Their decision was plain on their faces. They'd never do what Wayne wanted. He tried to catch Wayne's eye, but the "Colonel" wasn't looking at him.

The next delegates came in. They were three women in light blue outfits, not quite uniforms, but chosen carefully to give that impression anyway.

"Who let these scum in?" Sarge growled.

"Hey, ladies, don't mind Sarge there," Wayne said.

"I don't like being in the same room with you, either, Brezhinsky," one of the women snapped. Michael glanced at their eyes.

—*"We'll go," the woman said. "Time to get some of our own back."*
—*The desert. "Let them kill themselves," one woman said to the other. "Let's get out of here."*

Wayne looked at him. Well, he wanted to know the vote, right? Why tell him the rest? Michael nodded. Wayne grinned.

Finally, a group of six dark-skinned men and one grey-haired, bedraggled white woman, all dressed in black from hats to boots, sauntered in, laughing and joking with one another. "Eey, Wayne!" called a green-haired man. "Nice place!"

"Well, well," Sarge taunted. "It's the Nigger Army."

"Fuck you, old man," snarled Green Hair.

"Come on, gentlemen, no fighting in here," Wayne said nervously, clearly unaccustomed to keeping the peace. But both sides took their seats.

Wayne looked at Michael. He glanced over at the group.

—*"Hell with it," said one. "We're not going."*
—*Another walked through a strange jungle. The sky was a deep green.*
—*The third drove down a highway in a mag-van. Police were behind him.*
—*The fourth was having hot sex with the third.*
—*The fifth was sitting on his bed, reading a magazine. He missed the old days.*
—*The sixth sat in prison, wondering if anyone would ever come for him.*
—*The last flew through the skies of Valen.*

"Broken," he whispered. She glanced at him and smiled, giving him a little wave. What was she doing here? She seemed very pleased with herself.

He looked back at Wayne and shook his head *no*. Wayne's brows creased.

"Let's get started, then," he said.

The introductions took some time. It turned out that the old men in U.S. Army uniforms simply called themselves "The Corps," and were a hardcore separatist group. The women were militant supporters of the UNP, recently driven into the murky grasp of the underground. The men Broken was with were called the "North Jersey Anarchist Force" and seemed to be pretty easygoing, for anarchist revolutionaries. It was a bizarre mix.

Wayne started talking. "Friends, the time for action has come."

A few grumbled, but most paid attention as Wayne rose and paced around the room. His eyes were bright as he spoke. Michael wanted to shrink back from his sheer intensity, but dared not move.

"Comrades-in-arms, we have a purpose that we need to fulfill. We all know the crimes the government has committed on our beloved country. And now the government is fighting itself—"

The old man called Sarge stood. "I'm gonna talk," he growled. Wayne stopped mid-sentence, and sheepishly sat down, cowed by the grizzled soldier. "All right. This used to be a great country. America. That flag up there meant a lot of things to a lot of people. But the illegal 'United Nation' government has *sullied* what it once stood for!" He marched over to the three UNP women, who stared defiantly back at him. "Thanks to the Confederation, this is now one of the poorest, most backward places on the planet. Ever been to Australia? I have. The people there live lives of luxury, surrounded by shining technology. They refuse to share it! Dune Coons in Arab-Land get better junk than we do!"

The North Jersey Anarchist Force had a few things to say about his use of the term "Dune Coons," but the old man shouted them down. "I'm not finished! You can talk later! I'm not finished, damn it!" He huffed and puffed as his face turned a glorious shade of crimson. Michael hoped he might have a heart attack. "We used to have the best tech, the strongest army, the smartest men and the best government on the planet! What the hell happened?"

"The Last War, idiot," retorted one of the women. "President Greenleaf went crazy. Remember?"

"You're damn right I remember!" Sarge shouted in her face. She flinched. "I was there. I *fought* in that war. You weren't even a dirty thought in your old man's head yet! But I was there, I *know*. Everything they say about that war is a *lie*. We had to fight because Europe and China were ganging up on us! We had to protect freedom and democracy! And look what's happened since we lost! Crazy UNPers and aliens have been setting policy for the entire world, that's what!"

"A crazy man," one of the anarchists said, laughing.

"Shut up!" screeched Sarge. "Now it's time for us to get some of our own back, while the Confederation is busy eating itself! The Second American Revolution is on! We gotta take to the streets and recruit as many able-bodied young men as we can, right now! Then we gotta go back to the hills and strike 'em every day until we're a free nation again!"

The other old man clapped. Everyone else rolled their eyes. Wayne cleared his throat. "Sarge, we're here today to talk about taking the fight to the Confederation. If we bring down the government, we'll all be free! Right?"

"Right," echoed a few of Wayne's men.

"I ain't done yet!" Sarge bellowed. "I ain't done."

They waited. "America!" he cried, pumping a fist in the air. Then he sat down, winded.

"I guess he's done," said an anarchist. His group giggled.

"So," said one of the women. "Australia. Are we going?"

"Let's talk about it," Wayne said.

"Let's not," the anarchist leader replied. "We're staying put."

"Then why did you come to this meeting?" Wayne asked icily.

"Wanted to meet everybody," the green-haired anarchist grinned. "Maybe find some new trouble to cause. But Australia? No way. Dangerous."

"The fight is here," Sarge said, still breathing hard. "You should join up with us."

"You gonna call us 'coons?'"

"Naw, I save that for Ay-rabs only," he replied.

The anarchist leader shrugged. "All right, sounds like fun."

"Hang on!" Wayne said. "Hey. Hey, we need to go to Australia. I got transport and guns and everything. A bunch of other organizations are going, too! We're all going to land north of Terra City and march down there to take it over."

"How do you know other organizations are going? You talk to other people?" the UNP leader asked.

"No, I saw it on the Net," Wayne said. Everybody groaned.

"You idiot," Sarge said. "The Net is monitored by the government!"

"The Net is *run* by the government," one of the UNP woman said scornfully. "I should know. I used to work for them."

"Not *this* Net," Wayne said proudly. "It's something new. No one knows it exists but us."

"So how'd you find out?" an anarchist asked.

Wayne's smile drooped. "The original Net. But this

is the real deal!"

"Government can and does monitor all communications off or on a network," Sarge said. "The UNP did that. Lieberman Act, 2062."

"That was to help find Rogarian spies!" the UNP leader exclaimed.

"Yeah, well, that's what *you* say," Sarge growled.

"It would require millions of people looking through an unbelievable amount of information to look at *everything*," she insisted.

"You don't know shit. Why do you think they got big, fancy computers?"

"Look, look, just trust me... trust me, this is going to happen," Wayne said frantically. "We all have to go. There's going to be an army of tens of thousands!"

"ConFedForce has what, twenty million troops? Great plan!" laughed an anarchist. A few of his friends started clapping. Broken grinned and giggled.

"We expect support from the Army," Wayne said. "A lot of their generals used to be UNP."

"True," said the UNP woman. "That's the first reasonable point I've heard here."

"If we link up with them, we're unstoppable. Terra City isn't defended at all, so it'll be easy to take. Come on, are you all afraid of a fight?" Wayne asked.

"What?" howled Sarge, leaping to his feet. "I'll break you, boy, for saying that about me!"

"Well, are you coming?" Wayne taunted. "Or what?"

"This is insane," said an anarchist. "I ain't going."

"Then *stay*, coward," hissed Wayne. "And you too, old man! I'm going to Australia *tonight* to fight for freedom!" He pounded on the table. "I'm going to go fight for your freedom, you cowards, and you won't come with me!"

Sarge rose and advanced on Wayne. He stood toe to toe with him, staring him right in the eyes.

"Go get killed," Sarge recommended. "Do us a favor." With that, he and his buddy stormed out of the room.

"Well," the UNP woman sighed. "We might as well go with you. We have pretty good support down there; we ought to be able to at least link up with them. Better than staying here."

"How about you?" Wayne asked the anarchists.

Their leader shrugged.

"Nah, we're staying here. I said that. But we'll drink with you before you go, all right?"

Wayne smiled. "Yeah. That'd be nice."

—He had stolen all the anarchists' weapons and plunked them down in the hopper's hold. The anarchists were cussing him out from the tree to which they were tied.

"Not a bad idea," UNP woman said.

"Thanks," Wayne replied.

Michael wondered if he ought to warn them. Maybe later.

[CHAPTER 20]

SKY RANGER'S COMM CHIMED. HE sighed and toggled the switch. A man with an extremely thin face and a bent nose stared, vulture-like, back at him.

"Sir," Sky Ranger greeted him, automatically rising to his feet.

"I've located the boy," the thin-faced man said. He had a slight Australian accent. "He is with a specific-contact prescient and a speed-healer. They're in the woods of New Jersey."

Sky Ranger scratched his head. "Is this the same boy who you said—"

"Yes. I'm sending precise coordinates. Go alone."

"Another LED member ought to—"

"No. You alone."

Sky Ranger nodded. "Got it."

"And wear your new uniform."

"Yes, sir."

◆▷▶ ◀◁◆

The anarchists popped open a few beers with the UNP women and the American Liberation Army, and everybody sat around for an hour or two bitching about the government. Michael watched, transfixed, as they all slowly descended into drunken stupors. Wayne cursed and threw a few things, but overall he seemed to be feeling pretty good. Amazingly, Broken hadn't touched a drop, although she laughed and joked just the same as everybody else. She held a beer, but she never seemed to actually sip from it.

When they seemed out of it enough, he signaled subtly to her. She caught it on the first try, and nodded. He rose, praying that he was inconspicuous or they were too drunk to care, and edged slowly towards the door to the basement. No one stopped him as he opened the door and slipped into the stairwell. A moment later, Broken joined him.

He gave her a hug. "Good to see you. I knew you'd get out alive."

"Yeah," she said simply.

"Nice outfit." She was still wearing the black clothes the anarchists had given her; they set off her silver hair to stunning effect. She smiled. "Ian and Monica are downstairs." He led the way. Banner was sitting outside the door, looking very bored.

"Hey, Banner," Michael said.

"Hi, Mike," Banner replied. "Who's your friend?"

"Just someone I know. So, Banner, we need to get going."

"Oh. I thought you were under arrest."

"Well, not anymore. Can you open it up for me? Monica and Ian are coming, too."

Banner's eyes narrowed. "Says who?"

Michael sighed, and thought of ways to reason with him.

Broken put a pistol to his head. *Where'd she get that?* Michael wondered. "Please," she said.

Banner stared down the barrel of the gun for a full thirty seconds. He seemed to enjoy being right on the edge.

"Okay," he said finally. "You were nice to me, and I don't think Wayne is going to care."

"Nah," Michael said. Banner opened the door, and Monica, holding Ian, sprinted out, making sure to keep Michael and Broken between her and Banner.

"Thanks," Michael said, putting out a hand. Banner shook it. "Hey, when you're on board the hopper, remember, don't arm the bomb until it's in the air. Okay?"

Banner smiled. "I always had trouble with that in training. Thanks."

"No problem. You can sound the alarm whenever you like. Let's go."

Banner sat back down in his chair and waved as they ascended the staircase. "Goddamn, that was easy," Michael exhaled.

"Never easy," Broken reminded him, shaking her head. Overhead, they could hear the whine of a hopper's engines.

They burst through the door into an empty room.

Everyone had rushed outside at the sound of the incoming aircraft. Broken still had her pistol; she checked the clip and held it at the ready.

Michael led the way. He poked his head out the front door of the cabin. A gray, beat-up hopper settled gingerly onto the lawn. The anarchists had already been tied to the tree; their weapons were in the hands of the American Liberation Army and the UNP women, who had begun to climb into the hulking hopper.

"We can sneak away," Michael said, grateful for the convenient distraction. "They won't see." They trotted lightly away from the house. They were halfway to the forest edge when Ian decided to let out an ear-piercing shriek.

Crap.

All heads turned their way. "Hey!" Michael could hear Wayne shout.

A white-hot bolt sizzled past him, detonating at the treeline. Several sharp cracks followed.

"Stop!" called Wayne. "I won't miss next time!"

They froze. Wayne had already covered most of the ground between them, running full tilt. The plasma rifle he was carrying was trained on Michael.

"Fucking ungrateful son of a bitch!" Wayne screamed. "I take you in and *feed* you, and you *run away!*" He slowed to a trot and carefully aimed the plasma rifle. "You're dead. Got anything to say before you become a cinder?"

Michael had never seen this moment before.

Broken's head jerked up. Her mouth formed an 'O'.

"Wayne!" several of his comrades were calling, panic in their voices. "Wayne! Come back! Hey!"

Wayne looked up at the sky and started back. "Oh, fucking shit!" he said, eyes wide. He took off at a dead run towards the hopper.

Michael scanned the vast blue sky, squinting against the weak winter sunlight.

He finally made out what they had seen. A man, flying without any vehicle, bearing straight towards them.

"Sky Ranger," he breathed.

Someone grabbed his arm. He turned to find Broken staring, horrified, up at the approaching figure.

"Oh, no," she whispered. "No, no. No. Please."

"Come on," Michael urged. "The woods. He can't see us there."

"No," Broken said, her voice shaking. "He always finds who he's looking for."

"Run *anyway*," said Michael, pulling her.

Monica clutched Ian. "Oh, Jesus, I see him," she wailed. "Let's go!"

"No," murmured Broken. "I'm staying." She walked forward.

"B!" Monica called.

"Come on!" Michael made up his mind, grabbing Monica and bolting towards the woods.

The trees were getting closer. He felt like his lungs would burst. Monica clung to his hand with the arm that wasn't cradling Ian.

A *whoosh* of air almost knocked them down. When they managed to look up, a huge, powerfully built man, black cape swirling around him, blocked their path. Under the cape, he wore the uniform of a Black Bands commander.

"Your government needs that baby," he said,

pointing a gloved finger at Ian.

Monica held him close, falling to her knees.

"No," said Michael. "You'll turn him into a monster."

"You don't understand, son," Sky Ranger said, not unkindly, "He's special. He can do great things. He can be such a boon to humanity. He'll be our strength."

"I know that," Michael told him. "He's going to save humanity from *you*."

Sky Ranger shook his head. "I don't have time for this. I need to take him now. I won't hurt you, and I don't need you. You're free to go."

"Maybe... maybe you should go away," interrupted Broken, walking forward. Her face had a strange expression on it, glazed and faraway, as if she was looking at a different scene entirely.

"Go away," he commanded, barely glancing at her. "This doesn't concern you."

"Little Hawk," she whispered. "It does."

Sky Ranger's eyes grew wide as he took her in. After a long moment, he began, "You..." and broke off, studying her intently.

She stood there, subjecting herself to his scrutiny, her face unreadable.

Sky Ranger forced a smile. "Hey... so it *was* you! Silverwyng."

Broken looked stricken. "Yeah," she managed. "I don't go by that name anymore."

"I've missed you. Did you know that?"

A light gleamed in her eyes. "... Really?"

"Of course! We all did. It was terrible. First Crim died, then you vanished, then Lucky left... Do you remember?"

She nodded, speechless.

"You shouldn't have gone, Sil. You should come home to the Tower. Come back with me now."

"No. I don't think I want to..."

"Well, you have to," he said, voice low and persuasive, almost beguiling. Michael himself wanted to do what he said, go where the imposing man commanded. "You're in violation of the law, sweetheart. Both of you are." He glanced at Michael. "You're a Prescient, I've heard."

"I'm a what?" Michael asked, stunned. "Broken..."

"Is that what you're calling yourself? 'Broken'?" Sky Ranger laughed. "Sil, you're not broken."

"I can't fly," she said, close to tears. "I used to be able to fly."

"I bet Doc can help. He's still there, you know. He was so worried when you left, and then Lucky went away not long after. Were you with her?"

Broken looked at the ground. "Jane's dead."

"Oh." Sky Ranger sighed. "I see. Look... I have to take the baby. And you, Sil, you can come with me, too."

"Um," Broken stammered, torn. "I..."

Michael looked at Sky Ranger, and saw cold calculation behind his bright eyes and loving smile. He opened his mouth to speak, but the leader of the Union beat him to it.

"Sil." He reached out to her. "Come back to me. Fly with me again."

She looked into his ice-blue eyes, and walked to him, as if in a trance. He gently took her arms.

"You'll come home with me," he said softly. "You were always welcome to come home."

Michael shook his head. "This isn't fair," he said simply. "Broken..."

She detached herself. "I'm sorry. Michael, I'm sorry. I want to go home. I... I'm sorry." She gently took Ian from Monica's arms.

"Don't listen to him, Broken," Michael warned, but he knew it was too late.

"Traitor," Monica hissed.

"Sorry," Broken repeated. Ian wiggled, but did not cry. He trusted Broken. She carried him to Sky Ranger's waiting arms. He cradled the child in one arm and took her in the other, then, with visible effort, lifted himself off the ground.

"Hold on," he told her.

"Broken!" Michael called desperately.

She didn't look at him. Instead, she looked across the sloping lawn at the hopper, still idling and ready for takeoff. The American Liberation Army had fled inside it, hoping not to be noticed.

"Goodbye," she called, still not looking at Michael. Instead, she gazed up into Sky Ranger's handsome face. He smiled down at her.

"You did the right thing," he said. "Good for you."

He lifted up into the air, and moved off towards the east.

"No!" cried Michael. "No! Come back!"

Broken looked back at him as Sky Ranger sped into the distance... and, finally, he saw what she was planning.

Monica was crying. "How could she? I don't understand!"

Michael looked around wildly. There, far across the lawn, the hopper still idled. He ran towards it, waving his arms and shouting.

"Hey!" he called. "Hey! Open up!"

A hatch popped open. Wayne, Parker, Banner, Kent and the others glared at him, weapons pointed at his head.

"Fuck off," Kent said.

"Please, you need to help," Michael said. "That baby is the best chance we have for the future. He's the only one who can take Peltan down. Please! Please, help me!"

Monica ran up behind him, wheezing.

"We're going to Australia," Wayne said, voice shaking a little. The close encounter with Sky Ranger had rattled him.

"To do what? Die? No one will remember you when you spill your blood out on the sands, *no one*. It won't matter. You help me save Ian, you'll have saved the entire fucking world." Michael stared defiantly at them. "Please," he said again. "Please."

They looked at each other hesitantly. "I don't know," said one of the UNP women.

"Yeah," agreed another. "This is stupid. We should go."

Michael pointed. "*They're* planning to run away the first chance they get. Don't trust 'em."

"You rat!" said one of the women.

Wayne glared at them. "Is that true?"

Their leader pulled a pistol and pointed it at Wayne's men. "Shitheads." She and her compatriots carefully backed out of the hopper and were gone.

Wayne turned to Michael. "You're sure, about the kid?"

"Yes!" Michael pleaded. "They're getting away! We don't have much time!"

"What is it?" demanded Monica. "What's happening?"

"Broken is planning something. We have to go *now*, though, or it won't work."

Wayne looked at his troops.

"We should," Banner said. "It's the right thing to do."

"Damnit, Banner, you..." Wayne cursed. "So fucking naïve!" But he was smiling. "All right!" he yelled. "Lift the fuck off! *Let's bring down Sky Ranger!*"

He ran to the cockpit and strapped himself in. With a sickening lurch, the hopper leapt into the sky.

"Towards the city," Michael instructed.

"Yahooo!" shrieked Wayne as the hopper sped off in hot pursuit.

◆►◄◆►

The wind whipped through her hair, the cold breeze chilled her face and hands... Sky Ranger's strong arm was wrapped solidly around her.

"Hey," she called, the air carrying her words away. "Hey!" She looked up at him.

"Hold tight," he said, grimacing.

"I've missed you," she said.

"Yeah."

"Did you really miss me?"

"Sure."

She struggled with herself, plans coming and going. "Well... if that's true... why didn't you ever come looking for me?"

"Can we talk about this later?" he grunted. "It isn't

easy to do this."

"It was for me," she said. He pretended not to hear.

She had carried him, when they made love in the sky. He lost control, and she held both of them up. She did it without thought, without effort.

"*Did* you come looking for me?"

"Well, sure. But you were hard to find."

"How did you find us this time?" she asked.

He said nothing.

"Hey, I see them!" Parker pointed. A little speck floated off in the distance, zipping towards New York City.

"Yeah, that's gotta be them," Kent said, clutching his rifle to his chest. "We're gaining."

"Where'd you get this thing?" Michael asked.

Wayne laughed, high and shrill. "Kent *stole* it from a *hospital!*" He giggled uncontrollably.

"What are you going to do with the baby?" she asked.

"Huh?" Sky Ranger seemed incredibly distracted.

"The baby. Is he coming to live with us?"

Sky Ranger shook his head.

"I have to take him to Australia. Orders." He sighed. "You don't need to know about that."

"Okay," she said.

Below, she spied the coastline, and the sea...

The sea.

She looked at Ian's huge black eyes. He stared back at her, and she saw the future reflected there.

She glanced back. A small dot showed against the sky. A hopper?

The sea. A tide pool...

Memory seared her, leaving foresight behind.

Sky Ranger never loved her. He never would. He'd lock her in the Tower for the rest of her life. She'd never be free again.

The dot was growing larger. Following them. Following... *Michael*. He had picked up on what she had sort of been planning all along. Of course.

After that, the choice was easy.

"Sky," she said, tears blinding her. "Sky, I'm sorry."

"What?" He seemed irritated. "Now what?"

She brought her legs up and kicked his chest. Startled, his grip on her loosened... and Broken twisted free.

Sky Ranger was a little dark speck, growing ever larger. "I don't think he knows we're here yet," Parker said.

"Look!" Monica cried, grabbing Michael and pointing.

Something separated from the speck, hurtling towards the ground.

She grabbed for Ian as his arms loosened. But Sky Ranger was too quick, and she missed... and fell.

Broken watched Sky Ranger's face recede again.

Just like before... except this time, he just looked annoyed. He clutched Ian tightly, faced forward, and sped towards New York, leaving her to descend to earth alone.

No...

◄►► ◄►►

"Broken!" Monica screamed.

"I saw it, he didn't drop her," Parker said. "I saw it! She fought free of him."

"*Shiiiiit,*" Wayne breathed, watching her fall. "She's toast."

"She'll be fine," Michael said. "Sky Ranger..."

They scanned the sky. Free of his burden, the leader of the Extrahuman Union had, sped up and disappeared. Ian was gone.

"Find him!" Michael roared.

[CHAPTER 21]

WAVES WASHED OVER HER, PUSHING her destroyed body further into the sands.

The pain was a welcome respite from oblivion. She had come to hate and fear death more than ever these past few days. This time there had been no thrill of falling, only the bitterness of failure. She had hoped to delay him, maybe get him to drop *both* of them... she felt sure she could have protected Ian from the fall. No. He had turned his back on her, again. He had changed so much... but in some ways he was the same as always.

She felt saltwater seeping into the closing wounds on her legs and back, stinging like a thousand jellyfish.

She could smell again, and now she could hear. Gulls cried, the waves roared.

The sea.

She hadn't been to the sea since...

Pain forced a memory she had kept in the dark her entire life forward.

"Hey, kiddo!" called the woman. "Come on, you'll be late!"

(No. She tried to push it away.)

A woman with red hair and a welcoming smile waved to her. "Sweetie, come on in, it's late!"

"Be right there, Mom!" she called.

(Mom?)

She wanted to pick a shell out of the bottom of the tide pool. She reached in, but something big moved towards her. She recognized the blue crab, but didn't withdraw her finger soon enough.

With a swipe of its claw, it snipped off the tip of her finger.

(This is it. Steady now.)

She yelped in pain and surprise.

Her mother ran as fast as she could. "What happened?! What..."

She opened her eyes and looked down. The ground was ten feet beneath her.

A sharp pain stabbed at her from her hand. She looked at her finger. It was growing back.

"Oh, come down, honey!" called her mother. "Oh, no, no, no..."

She looked back at her mother, who started to cry in despair.

"Oh, Penny..."

❖❖

Her eyes snapped open.

Michael, Monica, Wayne and the others stood over her.

"Fucking shit," said Wayne. "She really did survive."

"Broken," Michael said. "How are you?"

She smiled. It hurt, but she couldn't help herself.

"I remember now," she whispered. "My name is Penny."

❖❖

They sat on the beach as night fell, illuminated by the hopper's searchlight. Kent had started a fire, on which they had cooked some of the meat the militia had provisioned for the journey. Broken ate ravenously. She could hardly speak, except to apologize over and over.

"I'm so sorry," she said again. "If I hadn't... "

"He'd have taken Ian anyway," Michael reassured her. "You did your best."

"Did you see it coming?" she asked.

He smiled. "Yes."

She nodded. "I'm glad."

"I'm glad you didn't betray us," Monica said. "I'm sorry about what I said."

Broken nodded, but didn't respond. She had been closer to betraying them than she liked to admit.

"Still. He's got Ian now, and we'll never get into Union Tower," Monica said sadly. "They'll be waiting for us. I guess it's over."

Broken straightened up. "Oh. Oh, he told me. They're not going to the Tower. He's taking Ian to Australia."

At the mention of Australia, the American Liberation Army, all five of them, perked up.

"Yeah?" Wayne asked, suddenly interested.

She nodded. "He said it was 'orders.' "

Michael shivered despite the warmth of the fire. "The thin man," he breathed. "He's in charge of Sky Ranger. He must be taking Ian to him."

"Who's the thin man?" Monica asked.

"He's... I *think* he's like me," Michael said. "Only a lot stronger. He works for Peltan."

"So he knows what's going to happen, too?" Parker asked. "Sucks."

"I know," Michael agreed. "But... I haven't seen any futures where we don't have to face him. I... I still don't. We have to go to Australia. We have to. I know where. There's a place north of Terra City... I should be able to find it. I've seen it so many times..."

"To Australia..." Monica murmured. "I don't know... can we survive if we go there?"

"Maybe," Michael said. "I don't know. There has to be a chance."

"Forgive me for saying it, but you've been wrong before."

He grimaced. "I know. I guess I'm not that reliable after all. Maybe you shouldn't follow me."

Broken put a hesitant hand on his shoulder. He started at her touch. "I trust you. I'll go. We'll swim if we have to." Her gray eyes were bright and sincere. A breeze spun her silver hair around her face; in the firelight, she looked ethereal, angelic, powerful.

"Thanks," he managed to say.

Wayne leaned in. "There going to be fighting there?"

Michael nodded. "Most definitely."

"Cool," Wayne said, grinning fiercely. "Count us in." He looked utterly mad in the light of the flickering flames.

After a moment, Banner nodded soberly.

"Yeah," he said. "Count us in." The others muttered their agreement.

Monica sighed. "I never wanted to see thirty anyway," she said. "All right. Let's go."

The hopper lifted off the sand, leaving only the remains of a fire and an eroding dent in the sand where Broken had crashed.

Aboard the hopper, Michael sat, lost in nervous thought. Wherever he looked, he saw the thin man. He saw death.

He couldn't escape it now.

[CHAPTER 22]

THE BULKY GRAY HOPPER SOARED OVER the landscape, eating up the miles between New Jersey and Australia. Michael and Wayne passed the time by poring over a map of the continent.

"We can land outside the northern suburbs," Michael said, jabbing the map with his finger. "Sky Ranger probably took Ian to this ConFedMil complex outside the city. I think that's what I've been seeing lately. It's surrounded by desert scrub, so it's north of the city somewhere."

"We can land north of Tenser Field," Wayne said. They both went silent for a moment at the mention of the name. Tenser Field, where the Räton ship *Mathapavanka* had landed more than fifty years ago, changing humanity forever.

"Alien scum," Wayne spat, though a hint of awe

tinged his voice, belying his words.

"They brought good as well as bad," said Michael. "More good than bad, if you ask me."

"Cultural degeneration," Wayne sneered, unconsciously borrowing a phrase from the Reformists. "Twenty thousand dead in the war against the Rogarians, which *they* dragged us into, not to mention 'Rattie' control of the government. That's good? You're fucked up."

Michael shrugged. "They gave us colonies. That's good."

"Why? Who needs colonies?"

"It spreads us out," Michael said grimly. "We can't all be destroyed at once."

Wayne looked genuinely thoughtful. "Huh. Never thought about it like that. Yeah, maybe they're good. But the Ratties as a whole have been shit for us."

"I've never even seen one," Michael admitted.

"Nah. Me neither. Kent did, once. Ask him to describe it, he tells it real funny."

Michael sighed and changed the subject. "We're going to see if we can sneak into the place when we get there. We might not have to."

"Can we blow it up? 'Cause I got all *kinds* of stuff to do that here." Wayne grinned, then leaned back and started humming a nameless tune. He seemed a lot more relaxed. Maybe heading off towards certain death agreed with him. Michael was nothing but tension.

On the other side of the cabin, Monica and Broken conversed in hushed tones.

"... So I bailed out. I was hoping he'd come after me or drop Ian, which would mean he'd have to go chasing after him. Then you guys could catch up."

"You could see us?"

"A little. I figured it was you." She pointed at Michael. "*He* has his ways."

"He really does, doesn't he... I wonder why he's doing all this? He doesn't seem to like people very much. Why save them?"

"Because he can," Broken said simply.

Wayne looked at the map again. "It's gonna be hot, huh."

"Yeah," Michael said. "Summer, there."

"Oh, yeah. I forgot. Guess I better ditch the coat, right?" He laughed. "So tell me, prophet-boy, did you see any of this coming?"

Michael shook his head. "I wish I had ten credits for every time someone has said that to me. No, not really. I didn't see Broken handing Ian to Sky Ranger, not until it was happening. I didn't see us working with you. I may have seen a flash of it here or there, but I don't remember everything I see. The future has millions of possibilities, and I only see a fraction of them."

Wayne cackled again. "If anything can happen, what's the point of seeing the future? It's all random!"

Michael laughed with him. "You know? You have a point there."

Monica leaned closer to Broken. "Hey, can you tell me? What's death like?"

Broken thought. "It really isn't like anything. I don't know."

"... Does it hurt?"

She nodded. "Sure. Unless it's really quick." She looked away. "Coming back hurts more."

"When you were dead... did you see anything?"

Broken shook her head. "It's like sleep, but no dreams. Oblivion. But I'm not *really* dead. I'm still in my body, if that's what you're asking. I don't go anywhere because I always come back. So *real* death is probably different, because you go somewhere else."

"Broken," Monica breathed, "You believe in the soul?"

Broken looked at her as if she had grown another head. "Of course."

"Where... where do you think we go when we die?"

Broken shrugged. "Away. Somewhere that isn't here."

That made sense. Monica sat back and absorbed it. "You believe in God, Broken?" she asked.

Broken thought for a while. "Maybe," she said slowly. "Maybe."

Michael looked out the window, but there was nothing but darkness beneath. Hours to go. The hopper wasn't very fast.

Still, they weren't being chased, not as far as they could tell. That was a good thing.

Monica sat down next to him. "All right?" she asked.

He nodded. "It isn't going to be easy when we get there."

"You see that?" she asked teased gently.

"Don't have to be a prophet."

"But you've seen this, or at least a bit of it, before, right?"

"Yeah," he admitted.

"What did you see?"

"Lots of things. So many things." He heaved a shuddering sigh. "There's... there's a man waiting for me there, I think. A tall, thin man. I think he's going to kill me."

Monica frowned at him. "Then why are you going?"

Michael looked away. "I have to."

"Does it have something to do with your grandfather?"

"So you're the prescient now?" Michael snapped.

She smiled tolerantly. "I just guessed. But am I right? Is it because of him?"

"Joe wasn't my grandfather. He took me in when my parents died."

"Why?"

"Because." His worst suspicions came to the surface. "Because I had to do this, I think. He wanted to get me ready. He had seen Ian coming... for years. He was like me, but stronger. He could see all kinds of things. He knew I'd need him. He knew I'd go find Ian someday if he took care of me..."

"So, what, then? He trained you?"

"Not exactly. I mean, he taught me what my powers were. But I think he thought he'd be around to help me get Ian, so he didn't tell me a lot of things I could have used. But..."

Monica waited patiently, sympathy etched into her face.

"He died. He died before he thought he would. So I had to go on alone. He didn't see it coming." Michael shook his head.

◄►►◄►►

Joe lay on his bed in their cramped apartment, struggling to breathe. He had refused to go to the hospital. "All my futures are black now," he had said. "No point in delaying."

"You said you wouldn't go so soon," Michael said, fighting back his tears.

"I know. But sometimes... sometimes the craziest things happen instead of the things you expect. That's what makes this so hard."

"What will I do?" Michael asked.

"Go on. You could find that boy. You've seen him."

Michael nodded, sniffling. "Yes."

"You don't have to do it. You know that."

"I know."

"But it's important. We can't fix any of what's happening now..." He gestured to the screen. The election. Damian Peltan was winning. Black Bands were celebrating. The UNP was defeated. Darkness was spreading.

"The people have made a very bad choice," Joe said, "And they'll pay for it. But that boy... he's hope, before we have any right to hope. He's an early way out. Does that make sense?"

Michael nodded. "I know."

"But it's your choice. It's dangerous. If they catch you... if they get their hands on him, he'll be a monster. It'll make things so much worse. And it's such a slim hope anyway..."

"I'll do it," Michael said.

Joe grunted, satisfied. "I know you will."

They sat together in silence for a few moments. Then: "Joe," Michael said. "Why did you take me in? Was it about that boy? What about my parents? Did you even know them? Was it...?" He couldn't ask the rest.

But Joe had fallen asleep. The next time he woke, Michael couldn't bring himself to ask any of it.

"I just can't believe it's all gone," Monica was saying. "Back there. My home and my family. I keep thinking, won't Andrew think this is strange when I tell him about it, but I won't... I won't tell him. Because he's dead. Jane is dead. Shawn... Fred. Even Lyddie. I just can't believe it."

"Janeane isn't dead," Michael said.

"How do you know that?"

"I just do."

She looked at him. "Prophecy? You see that?"

He shook his head. "Janeane is special. I think I'd know if she died."

An hour later, they were flying over the wide Pacific, and everyone was starting to get tense, almost itchy.

"The government will be able to see us coming," fretted Michael. "We're going to be shot down before we even get close."

"We've got some stealth tech on this thing," Parker said.

"On a hopper you stole from a hospital," said Michael. "Right."

Wayne rolled his eyes. "We put the stealth tech on *after*, dick-nar. What did you think? Stealth ambulance?" He sniggered. "That'd be great."

"They'll probably think we're a sensor blip or something," Parker said. He seemed to be a lot more sober and technical-minded than the others. "At least, that's what I'm hoping. There's a lot of air traffic around Terra City. If we stay out of restricted zones, we might be okay."

"That's the spirit," grumbled Kent.

"I didn't think of restricted zones," Michael admitted. "We might have to land somewhere farther away."

"That's okay," Wayne grinned. "We're up for some walking."

Michael went back to the map. He glimpsed Broken looking out a window at the lights of South Africa twinkling in the distance. They'd be crossing the terminator into day, soon.

"Hey," he said, walking over to her. "How are you doing?"

"Okay," she replied. "I've never left North America. I wonder if Australia is really different?"

"I don't know," Michael said. "Probably."

He looked out the window. He could see the waters streaming by below. "Nice view."

"What's going to happen to Ian if we don't get him back?" Broken asked.

"They're not going to hurt him or anything. They'll just raise him to be... well, just like them. Maybe worse. That's what I've seen." He didn't mention the bloody coup he'd witnessed, nor did he mention the bodies in the street, the executions, the savagery of Ian's rule... "They won't treat him badly. But it would be bad for humanity, and for the other races like the Rätons, too."

"And if we save him and take him to Valen, he'll be good for humanity?"

"Right. I've seen him leading a rebellion against Peltan, then bringing all three races together in peace. Rätons, Rogarians, and us, one nation. It's amazing." Michael smiled. He liked those visions. He didn't see them much anymore.

"It sounds nice. Will we see it?"

He shook his head. "I won't. You might be a little old lady. It won't happen for a long time."

"Oh." She frowned. "So we might never know if it would really happen or not."

"That's the problem with the future," he said. "You never know how it's going to turn out unless you live long enough to get there. It's all a gamble. That doesn't stop anyone, though. We're always trying to have an impact on the future. Isn't that why people have kids, or teach, or build something, or save money? Except that we don't know whether it will happen or not. The planet could explode the next day; no one would know. It's crazy."

"Maybe..." she started.

"What?"

"Maybe we have faith in the future. That it will happen and it will be better than today. Hope. Maybe that's why."

"Yeah. Something like that." Michael said, smiling. "You've been talkative lately. I like that."

"I don't know why. I never was before. It's strange."

"Does it matter?" he asked. "Remembering your name?"

She nodded happily. "To me it does. It's like I'm more alive."

They sat together for a few more minutes, enjoying each other's companionship. There was no need to speak, not now. Then Michael stood, sighing. "I need to go look at the map."

She nodded and went back to looking out the window. Strange. For the first time in forever, she was looking forward to what tomorrow might bring.

Life. They picked up speed over the ocean, racing the sun towards Australia.

[CHAPTER 23]

THEY SAW A FEW OTHER BULKY HOPPERS, tiny, fast zippers, ancient planes, and long, looming liners as they streaked towards Australia's east coast, but the real traffic picked up as soon as they crossed over the shoreline.

"There must be hundreds of ships in the sky," Parker said. "This is amazing. It never gets this busy over New York." Below, a vast metropolis spread from the sea inland, towards the mountains.

"Big business and government are all in Australia," Michael explained. "Lots of people here with important stuff to do."

"I can't *wait* to blow some of 'em up," growled Wayne, eyes afire. "Bam!" He giggled. "Bam, bam, bam! Yeah!"

They cleared the mountains, and gradually the cultivated lands gave way to flat, featureless desert. They were getting close—Terra City lay on land reclaimed from the Outback.

"Try to find a public lot outside the city," Michael told Parker. "They shouldn't give us too much trouble."

"Yeah, maybe. But we should leave most of our weapons here."

"What!" exclaimed Wayne. "No! That's crap!" He grabbed for his gun.

"Just for appearance's sake!" Parker said quickly, backing off. "We're going to be walking through the suburbs! We can bring pistols, grenades, subtle stuff, stuff we can hide—but no rifles. Please don't shoot that in here. You'll have plenty of time to do it later."

"Shit," Wayne said, slumping down in his chair.

They were getting closer to Terra City. Expressways and massive aqueducts crisscrossed the desert; green fields began to dominate the landscape. It had been scrubland and dry riverbed fifty years before; then Räton agricultural technology and shifting weather patterns had made the desert bloom. Now Australia was the world's breadbasket, while the Mississippi Valley dried and withered on the vine.

The hopper's traffic-adjustment sensors and computers were working overtime trying to keep them out of the way of all the other incoming and outgoing sky traffic. "Attention!" an Australian-accented voice said. "Obey all traffic laws! Reduce speed to 200kph when approaching Terra City!"

"Just a broadcast traffic signal," Parker said, breathing a sigh of relief. He adjusted the speed of the hopper, while noticing that most of the other air traffic had ignored the warning.

"Try not to stick out," Michael said.

Parker nodded. "Man, these other airs look great, don't they? All shiny and new. I wonder what *that* cost?" He pointed to a brilliantly colored, sleek new zinger.

"Bet I could steal it," Kent bragged.

"Do us a favor and *don't* try," Parker said. "Hey, we're over the suburbs."

"Good. Start looking for a place to land," Michael said.

Parker maneuvered down into the lower, more local traffic levels. "Where are we?" he asked. "I'm lost." Acre after acre of newly built suburban landscape stretched out below. The houses were all large, with lots of land.

"Maybe not here," suggested Michael. "Somewhere more public."

Wayne tried to read the map. "Shit, I have no clue where we are." Michael looked at his screen. They had made it nearer to the ConFedMil facility than he'd dared to hope. Only a dozen miles or so.

He caught a glimpse of his own reflection in the screen.

—The thin man stood at the entrance. "I've been waiting for you," he said. The men around him opened fire.

"Set down anywhere near here," he instructed, pushing the vision away. He glanced up at the streams of air traffic heading for Terra City, and briefly wondered about the vast, modern city. He'd only ever seen it on screens, and a part of him wanted to explore it. All the monuments, and the massive government house. He couldn't afford to be a tourist, though.

Parker set the aircraft down in a grassy public hopper lot on the edge of a sprawling commercial center. Their hopper was the oldest and ugliest in the lot.

"Camouflage!" Kent shouted, looking around. "Awesome."

"It'll do," agreed Banner, but he didn't sound so sure. Wayne and Parker said nothing, although Parker looked nervous.

"Okay," said Michael. "Should we try to find transportation, or walk?"

"You know how to get there?" Kent asked.

Michael shrugged. "North. That's what I remember. I think there's only one road north."

"Then we either take the bus or ask a cop for directions. Which would you rather?"

Good point. "All right," he said. "Everybody out."

The first thing that struck them was the intense heat. Changes in weather patterns and a massive aqueduct system engineered to bring water to what was once desert hadn't changed the fact that the South Australian summer was brutally hot and dry.

"I need a drink," griped Wayne. "And not the fun kind."

"I think we're going to need to save our water," Michael said. He looked around at the other people coming and going from the lot. No one was really looking at them, but a lot of them wore Reformist pins on their lapels. A few wore the black-and-white armbands of the Black Bands Reserve.

Not a good sign.

They took what they could from the hopper, carefully concealing as many weapons as they could in their packs, and headed off towards a transport station in the center of the commercial complex.

Vast and intimidating, the complex was hard to navigate. Rows and rows of expensive-looking shops, most containing fashionable clothes or unfamiliar gadgetry, seemed to stretch on towards infinity. Everywhere, well-to-do members of the Australian governing class strode busily past with bundles of goods, or chatting loudly into a mini-screen. No one seemed very friendly; in fact, most of the people they passed seemed tense and jumpy.

Wayne, Kent, Parker, and Banner had lost their bluster. They seemed subdued and nervous, cowed by their surroundings like the provincials they were.

"Fucking 'Roos," muttered Wayne. "So fucking full of themselves."

"Shh," cautioned Michael, glancing around apprehensively. No one seemed to have heard. Thankfully, the transport station was just up ahead; they just had to make it a little farther.

"Look," whispered Monica, turning pale. All over the commercial complex there were posts with happy messages like "Summer Holidays" or "Enjoy Shopping." On the post nearest them, though, a dead Räton hung.

"My God," Michael said, trying not to stare. "Is that..."

It had green skin, and wild blond growths that looked like hair. Everyone always said that Rätons looked so much like humans... but Michael hadn't realized how much until now.

"Looks real," Broken said, pointing to a puddle of bluish-green blood on the ground. The alien had been gutted and strung up. Its huge, deep amethyst eyes held an expression of surprise and sadness. A cardboard sign reading "ALIEN SCUM" was tied around its neck. Next to its head, a banner reading "Happy New Year 2107!" fluttered in the breeze.

"Shit," Wayne breathed. "Shit. Shit."

"Let's keep moving," Michael said in a low voice. "Don't want to attract attention."

There was more gallows fruit ahead. On another lamppost hung two humans, a man and a woman. "TERRORISTS" was scrawled across their signs. Their faces were purple; their tongues, swollen and blue, hung out of their mouths. A puddle of piss and shit lay festering beneath each. Monica pressed a hand to her mouth.

"That could be me," she squeaked, clutching Michael's arm.

"Steady," he said, but he shook a little, too, in the face of such casual, thoughtless violence. Other people passed by the lamppost, obliviously shopping and chatting. Michael swallowed his disgust and dread.

They pressed on. The transport station was close.

A huge screen had been set up near the station. The usual good-looking announcers read the news.

"Breaking story, Jim," said the woman, her Australian accent lilting and sweet. "There are reports coming from Whyalla that seven more UNP terrorists have been captured, but a dangerous cell is still reported to be in the area of Port Augusta and Lake Torrens, south of Terra City. Citizens are urged to be vigilant, and to be mindful of their own safety. Another Citizen Alert: Citizens' Courts have been set up to judge the huge influx of prisoners in South Australia. If you think you have what it takes to serve the human race in this capacity, please volunteer! Many positions are available. Contact your local Ministry of Justice station for more information."

The man gazed solemnly into the camera. "In other news, President Peltan has issued an executive order in which he states that, in the absence of the Senate, he will personally enact needed legislation. All policies and laws created by the executive during this time will be subject to Senate approval when the new Senate convenes in a few months. The old Senate was dismissed earlier this week on the grounds that an unspecified number of opposition Senators were insurgents and terrorist supporters."

The woman beamed. "President Peltan assures the public that everything is being done to protect civil liberties as well as the safety of all citizens. In sports, Canberra—"

Michael groaned quietly, hoping that no one nearby would hear.

"Yeah," Monica agreed. "I thought it was bad at home, but it's a lot worse here."

Michael and Wayne checked out the map on the wall of the transport center. Passenger hoppers and ground buses were filling up and departing rapidly, mostly heading south towards the city. Stationed at the entrance to the gate, however, were several severe-looking Black Bands, backed up by a pair of regular police.

Michael ran his finger along the map. "Newcombe," he said. "That's where we are? Huh. That base should be only a few miles north of here. Lucky landing, Parker."

"Thanks," grinned Parker. "I try."

Despite himself, Michael found he was growing to like Wayne's crew of "soldiers." When they weren't kidnapping and trying to kill him, they were actually pretty nice guys.

"Instead of taking the bus, we should just walk it. What do you say?"

Everyone nodded. Wayne seemed a little put out. "Man, it's *hot*," he complained. But he straightened out his pack and laced up his boots while Michael tried to commit the map to memory.

"Okay," he said at last. "There's a street that runs parallel to this complex. If we follow it north," he pointed, "We should find it. Come on."

They tramped off. A few people stared at them as they walked away; try as they might to blend in, a motley crew like them, loaded with packs, was bound to stand out. A man with a black and white armband said a few words into a radio, and set off after them.

"These people have a lot of screens," observed Kent hungrily. "I mean, a *lot* of screens. Maybe I could take one, you know? They wouldn't even know."

It did seem like there was a screen broadcasting news, sports, or some other programming every few feet. People milled around watching one, then moved on to another to see what else was on. No one seemed to notice anyone else. It was eerie.

They finally emerged from the labyrinth of the shopping center and located the correct road, running off into the distance. They hiked across a vast grassy parking lot, on which endless rows of sleek, polished mag-vehicles rested. The road itself was a two-lane asphalt highway, on which both magnetic and wheeled traffic sped by.

"Try to keep on the grass," Michael suggested. They started north, panting in the intense heat. Michael felt sure he was getting a sunburn. There were few trees here, and little hope of shade. Behind the narrow strip of houses hugging each side of the road, farmlands stretched into the distance. Beyond the farmlands lay nothing but a vast expanse of parched, uninhabited scrubland. Civilization seemed to have settled on the South Australian interior like a fine dusting of snow. A few shifts here or there would melt it all away, leaving only the ageless desert to remember its passing.

They were right on the edge of Terra City's suburbs, close to the desert. Michael could taste dust whenever the wind blew.

That was right. He remembered dust and heat from his visions. Every step took him closer to Ian... and to the thin man.

—*The thin man shot Michael.*
—*The thin man shot Michael.*

**—The thin man laughed and showed Michael some-
thing he didn't want to see...**

In these visions, he no longer saw a path through
the thin man to any sort of victory. Still, Michael tried to
seem confident. What else could he do? They were here.
Too late to run now.

Or was it? Yet again, Michael warred with himself.
They trusted him. He could guide them to another location, declare it the site of his visions, and feign disap-
pointment at not finding Ian.

Then they could leave, and go back to their lives in
North America. Or, better yet, they could stay here. They
had nothing left at home.

Or... three tickets burned a hole in his pocket.
Broken, Monica, and Michael. Three tickets. They could
leave.

All they had to do was fly their stolen hopper back
to Delmarva, the departure point on the tickets, and get
on a ship bound for Valen.

Had Janeane planned it this way?

He twitched every time they passed a dirt turn-
off. We could do it there. There. There. Just work up the
courage. Don't walk into the lion's den.

Broken picked up on his mood. "Hey," she said
softly, so only he could hear. "When I was with the LED,
we got scared before we went out every time."

"You didn't know what was going to happen be-
forehand," Michael whispered back. "You don't know..."

"Like you said, though," Broken reminded him,
"You don't see what *will* happen. Only what *might*. So
the future's still up for grabs."

He shook his head. "Maybe," he said, unconvinced. Broken lapsed back into her usual silence.

One foot in front of the other. It was, he decided, easier to just keep walking straight ahead.

They walked for more than three hours without arriving at the base. The American Liberation Army was getting restive.

"Shit, I want to see some action," growled Kent. "Australia sucks."

"It's boring," Wayne confirmed. "Hey, Mike. When are we gonna shoot something?"

"Soon," Michael promised. He peered ahead, but could see nothing but endless road. The compound hadn't seemed so far on the map. Traffic was thinning out. The desert was clearly visible now, and there were far fewer houses lining the road.

A siren blared behind them. "Hey, you there!" a voice shouted. "Stop right where you stand!"

A police mag-car hovered behind them, lights flashing.

"Oh, shit," Monica said, edging back.

"Hold on," Michael warned as Kent and Wayne started moving. "Wait for my signal." They stopped.

Two men stepped out of the mag-car. One trained his pistol on Michael. "What's all this?" he asked. "You have ID? Let's see it."

Two possibilities diverged from here. Both led to the thin man eventually, but one was quicker. And here the moment came...

"No ID," Michael said. "Left it at home, sorry."

"A *foreigner*," hissed the cop. "And a *Yank* at that! Well, you're coming in with us. Get in there." He gestured with his gun.

The moment arrived.

"Now," Michael said quietly, and hit the ground. With a whoop, Wayne and his boys dragged out their guns and blazed away at the startled cops.

Michael saw flashes of plasma fire and heard the *crack* of bullets. Both officers fell with a thud, each a bloody mess.

"The car!" called Michael. "Let's go! Everybody squeeze in!"

They managed to pile into the police vehicle. Parker took the wheel; Michael and Wayne sat in the front. Kent, Banner, Broken, and Monica squeezed together in the back. "Go!" yelled Michael as soon as everybody was in. Parker hit the accelerator; the car lurched out onto the road. Wayne was screaming at the top of his lungs.

"Yah-HOOOOOO!" he called. "Yah! Yah! YAAAH!" He leaned out the window and fired his gun in the air.

"I—I think I killed one," Banner said, white as a sheet.

"Yeah, you did, buddy!" Kent beamed, slapping him on the back. Banner rolled down his window, leaned out, and puked up his guts.

"Glad he's in the window seat," Michael remarked calmly.

"Me, too," Monica said, face white.

◆►◄◆

Parker powered the car down the highway. The ride was smooth; they hovered on an electromagnetic cushion, and the acceleration and deceleration was controlled by manipulating the magnetic field. Some highways in North America were magnetic, but not many.

"This is a great road," Parker said. "Not many like it in Jersey."

"Yeah," Wayne said. "Nice and smooth. I love it!" His eyes were wild, his grin intense and more than a little crazed.

Michael stared down the road. As the sun set, it glimmered off the sand and asphalt, throwing off sheets of wavering light. They were really out in the desert now, no houses anywhere nearby and nothing but dust and rocks as far as the eye could see. The base had to be close.

They passed a sign. Michael barely had time to read it.

"Turn around!" he cried. Parker jerked on the wheel, and the car swung wildly around. When it stopped, they were pointing in the other direction. They were the only vehicle on the road.

"That road there," Michael pointed. "The base is there."

"You sure?"

Michael nodded. "Eyre Field. Go down there." Parker nodded and swung the car onto the road.

No one spoke. Michael's heart was beating fast. No one knew what would happen when they reached the end of this road, not even him. He glanced back at the others. Broken gave him a reassuring smile. Monica's head was lowered, and her lips were moving. A prayer?

Not the worst idea.

Michael remembered his visions. A huge, flat, concrete field, with a small, squat control building. That was all he could remember...

They crested a small hill—and there it was. The field was an ocean of concrete, dotted with control buildings here and there. It was entirely empty, save for one small spaceship crouched next to a lit control building. An electric shock of familiarity—and fear—coursed through Michael.

"That's it," he said, pointing. "That's where he is."

"How do we get in?" Monica asked. A high fence surrounded the place. "Is there a gate?"

"There," said Parker. A gap in the fence, bordered by two guard towers, stood near the ship and control building. "Can we get through?"

Michael knew the answer. He'd seen it sometimes. "Yeah. Floor it. They're not expecting anyone."

Parker shoved the car into high gear. The machine whined with power and surged forward. They raced towards the guard towers, sailing right between them. No one tried to stop them; there was no echo of gunfire, no running feet. Michael couldn't believe their luck.

"Head for that building!" he called. "Go!"

They roared towards the control building. "You sure about this?" Wayne asked.

"Trust me," said Michael. The police car screeched to a halt.

"Guns out!" called Wayne. "Move!" They poured out of the car and ran for the building. No one seemed to know they were there.

Michael prepared to knock down the door, but

found it open. He ran inside, followed by Wayne—

—And found himself face to face with ten Confederation soldiers. He skidded to a halt. The American Liberation Army pounded past him, and stopped dead.

The soldiers opened fire. Wayne, Kent, Parker, and Banner fell without a sound, without ever firing a shot.

No!

"Cease fire," commanded a calm, sharp voice.

Michael's mouth fell open; he started to shake all over. *He knew that voice.*

A tall, gaunt man wearing a Confederation Army uniform strode forward. Behind him floated Sky Ranger, still in the uniform of the Black Bands.

"Hello, Michael Forward," the thin man said crisply. He frowned. "I've been waiting for you."

[CHAPTER 24]

BEFORE HE COULD MAKE A MOVE, soldiers had bound Michael's hands. Broken and Monica were quickly restrained, as well. "Control room," the thin man ordered. "All three of them."

Michael glanced back. Kent, Banner, Parker, and Wayne lay motionless on the ground, riddled with bullets. Blood pooled around their eerily still forms.

"Wh... why did you kill them?" he demanded shakily. No one answered.

He hadn't seen that end for them. Had he? **The thin man's troops opened fire.** Could he have stopped it?

They'd followed him. Was it his fault they had died? His mind reeled. Beside him, Monica marched mechanically, in shock. Broken, on the other hand, was alert; her sharp gaze followed Sky Ranger's every move.

They were hustled down a flight of stairs, deep

into the warren of below-ground corridors that made up the majority of the base. The thin man calmly strode in front of them, silent and composed. Sky Ranger floated at his shoulder, attentive to his every move.

Michael felt like throwing up. This was it. This was *it*. Nothing could change what was going to happen now. He didn't even glance around to check. He knew there was no hope. Meeting the thin man was death.

At last, they arrived at a drab doorway marked "Command and Control." The thin man placed his thumb on a scanner, then typed in a code; the door slid back.

"Man your posts," the thin man told the soldiers. "And get rid of the bodies of the insurgents."

They saluted crisply and marched off. The door slid shut behind them, leaving Michael, Monica, and Broken alone with Sky Ranger and the thin man. Ian was no-where to be seen. Where were they keeping him? Not that it mattered. Ian's fate was all but sealed, Michael thought bleakly.

He stared at the floor, trembling, unable to think of anything worth saying. What was the point? All the possibilities now meant death.

The thin man regarded him with interest. "You shouldn't be so afraid, Michael. I have no intention of hurting you."

"You killed the people I was with," Michael retorted.

"Ah. Yes, they were armed and presumably danger-ous. These are not safe times; you of all people should know that. ...But it wasn't as if they mattered to you, is it? They were just a means to an end."

Michael kept his eyes fixed firmly on the ground.

"You've come quite a long way," said the thin man.

"And with very few resources! I'm impressed. Have you ever considered joining ConFedMilPol? That's the military police, technically, but the Administration has promised that we're going to be a lot more than just that in the future. And you know... we are. I've seen it. You understand *that*, I assume." He bared his teeth in a narrow, wolfish grin. "Sky Ranger here is going to join, as soon as his tenure with the Black Bands is done. Aren't you, Sky Ranger?"

Sky Ranger nodded. "It's an honor to serve, sir." He drifted to the ground and sat in a chair.

"You could be part of the Extrahuman unit we have planned. There wouldn't be very many, just a select few." He smiled. "I've seen you do just that, you know. I'm like you. I see—"

"I know," Michael said bitterly. "I've seen you say that a thousand times."

"Have you? ...I didn't realize I was so important to you. This must be a crossroads in your life, in one fashion or another."

"If you can see, you know it is," snapped Michael, straining at the bonds on his wrists. He was held fast.

"Yes. I *can* see, and far better than you in many ways. I see huge, general trends. I see the great span of history arching away down a thousand possible paths in front of us. I gather you can just see... details? And only when looking directly at a person involved?"

"Yes," Michael admitted.

"...What did you see when you looked at the boy? I'm curious."

Michael said nothing.

"I think I know what you saw. You saw two possible futures. One in which he grows up far away... on Valen, I believe... and another in which he is raised with us. You and I. Right?"

Still, Michael said nothing. *Yes.*

"Come now! I often have trouble seeing the details. I'd love to know what you saw. I've never met another Prescient, even one as different as you. Tell me."

Michael shook his head slowly.

"All right," said the thin man. He withdrew a pistol and shot Broken in the head. She crumpled to the ground, dead. Michael jumped, but still said nothing. Monica screamed. "Take her to a cell," the thin man instructed Sky Ranger. He nodded and scooped her up, ignoring her wails and kicks as they flew out the door.

"Now we're alone," the thin man said. "Oh, I know she'll wake up. She does. I've seen this moment, too, of course, and I've seen her. Remarkable sort of person. Very useful. Sometimes. So. Tell me. What did you see? The boy...?"

Michael studied the concrete for a while. The thin man adjusted a setting on his pistol and pressed it against Michael's palm.

"I have some flaws," he said conversationally. "One of them is extreme impatience, and a tendency to overreact when I don't get my way. It's all in my personnel file. So. When I fire this, it's going to burn your hand. The flesh will peel back and blister. Bone will show if I do it long enough."

Michael cleared his throat, still looking away. He hoped the thin man couldn't see him shake. "I saw... an alliance between the races. Us, the Rätons, and the Rogarians. He made it happen. There was peace... and everyone was free."

The thin man snorted derisively. "Oh, glorious. Freedom. Wonderful. And what else? The alternative?"

"I saw... him at the head of armies. He... he destroyed everything, everyone who stood up to him. Everyone hated him. Everyone feared him."

"Ah." The thin man regarded him, interested now. "Sorry about the threats," he said as he pulled the pistol away from Michael's hand. "I just need you to know how serious I am about all of this. ...And now, hearing you, I think I understand why you're doing what you are. It finally makes sense to me. You see these various futures from the perspective of individuals, not from the grand view of history. Let me tell you how I see it, shall I?"

Michael didn't want to hear, but listened anyway. What choice did he have? The thin man started to pace fitfully around the room, gesturing rapidly.

"If you had your way, he'd go to Valen and grow up to lead a rebellion against this government. He would cause anarchy and disorder in so doing. Yes, he would cobble together the alliance you spoke of, but it would last a mere hundred years, if that. A century only! Then chaos again. Warring states. Worse than now! That's the most likely path, there; I see few real deviations from it. And then? Who knows? The possibilities are too numerous to count. Chaos. It rarely turns out well for us, though.

"The other possibility, if we get our way—which we shall—runs like this. He will grow up to believe that humanity is great, that we have a magnificent destiny to fulfill. When he comes of age, he'll take the reins of government from that fool Peltan." He snarled as he spoke the president's name. "Peltan! A figurehead! A politician! A demagogue, really. Nothing but a political man driven by a child's ideology. Well, our boy will be something else. A new Alexander. A new Caesar. He'll *lead* us, oh yes. We'll grow stronger and stronger under his command, conquering planet after planet from our neighbors... he will be the emperor of mankind, and beyond!"

The thin man exhaled sharply, savoring the vision. "What a grand future! Humanity will be safe and secure, our enemies will be trampled underfoot—! Ah. Ah, yes. It's very satisfying, a lovely happy ending. Why is this *not* the preferable choice?"

"The people—" Michael began.

The thin man waved him off. "Yes, yes, some people will die. But they'd die in that rebellion of his, too, wouldn't they? And the chaos to follow?

"Yes, some liberties we had taken advantage of... they might disappear for a time. They might not return. Does it matter, though, really? Think, boy. If you were faced with the possibility of creating the new Rome, would you not do it? If you had an Augustus in your hands, wouldn't you use him to build that great empire? Or would you lead him against it, guaranteeing its destruction? Tell me, wouldn't it be worth the sacrifices to build a new Rome for humanity? All the horrible corruption of the past, all the insidious alien influences... all washed away. A perfect, brilliant state."

He smiled beatifically. "And now you know why I'm doing what I'm doing. I suppose it seems random and evil to you. It isn't. Both of us want what's best for humanity."

He stepped close to Michael, drawing his gaunt

face near Michael's cheek. "So. So! You could be part of our New Rome, if you want. It's your choice. Which would you rather? A century of peace? Or a thousand years of glory?"

He held the pistol to Michael's hand again. "Answer."

Michael raised his eyes to meet the thin man's.

—*"I'm sorry, Sky Ranger," said the thin man. "The Tower was destroyed by terrorist insurgents. I'm afraid there were no survivors."*

—*"I'm sorry, Sky Ranger," said the thin man. "Terrorists had barricaded themselves in the Tower, and the Union joined them. We had to destroy it."*

—*"I'm sorry, Sky Ranger," said the thin man. "The Tower was destroyed in an explosion earlier today. We don't know what happened. We suspect the Rätons."*

What?

Something new, even now?

He had never looked directly at the thin man. He had never read him. What did it mean?

"What are you going to do?" he breathed.

The thin man seemed confused for a moment. "Eh? Oh? Have you seen something?" He smiled. "Some wicked deed of mine, I take it?"

Michael shook his head, remembering to play his cards close for now.

The thin man sighed. "I wonder... How much of this conversation have you seen already? Do you see visions when you look in the mirror? Does it work like that?"

"Yes," Michael said.

"How upsetting!" murmured the thin man. "When my powers came upon me, I was a little boy, and it was most frightening. Was it like that with you?"

"Yes," said Michael again.

The thin man smiled again, this time more genuinely. "I must say, it is nice to have someone to talk to about... these things. You know. It's rather lonely, don't you think? And such power we have, such responsibility to try to set things right. I assume you didn't know old Val Altrera?" Michael shook his head, trying not to think about the letter he'd left back in the hopper. "Ah. Yes. Well. He was before your time. His visions nearly drove him mad before he and his loony followers went off to form their paradise on Valen. How strange, that you should want to go there! Perhaps there's a call... after all, you came to me. How odd indeed."

Michael watched the man move about the chamber, poking buttons and checking data on screens.

"What are you doing?" he asked.

The thin man pursed his lips. "You can't see for yourself? Your vision is that intermittent? How terrible for you; that must be truly inconvenient. We are going to move the government to Calvasna, and I have preparations to make." He laughed at Michael's expression. "Yes, I know, it's an odd thing to do, to move the capital to a colony world! But Terra City isn't safe, and, to be frank, the President doesn't really *like* it here. I don't blame him. So hot and dry... why *was* the city put here? Oh, yes, this was President Hampton's home state, was it not? Well, President Peltan is from Calvasna. The New Confederation can begin like the old did, in the home of its first ruler. And why not? Who will stop us? After this week, I think no one."

"Will you take Ian there?" he asked.

"Ian? Oh, do you mean the boy? You named him? That's a very sweet thing to do—no wonder you feel so strongly for him. Oh, yes, we'll take him. We're going to name him 'Alexander.' Do you think that's presumptuous of us? I don't. It makes sense, to those of us who can see the long view. He'll be Alexander Peltan; the President will adopt him, naturally. But *we'll* raise him."

The thin man raised his eyebrows, grinning twitchily, toothily, at Michael. "You can help with that. See him every day. You'd be able to anticipate more than I what his day-to-day challenges would be, keep him on the proper track. The President's other sons are... well, they're really not *fit*, you see. Best that little Alex be in charge when he grows up, instead of them. Yes, certainly."

"He will be," Michael said gamely.

The thin man threw back his head and laughed. "Ah-*ha*-ha! Well! Oh, you still think you can manage it... but that possibility is almost gone. I'm sorry. It can't be easy for you to let it go; you were so obviously attached to it. So. You can really only do two things, right now, my boy. You can join us, or not."

Michael shivered, not wanting to look into the thin man's eyes again. Not now.

"If—if I don't join you?"

The thin man shrugged, the motion awkward and jerky. "Oh? Well. I don't know. I won't shoot you! But it won't be all that nice, either. You won't be set free, even if you do join. Loyalty must be earned, I'm afraid. If you decide against it... even I can't say what will happen to you. But they'll never let you be a free man again. They might even kill you."

Slowly, hesitantly, despairingly, Michael glanced into the thin man's eyes.

A thousand possibilities unfolded. In each of them... Ian became Alexander. Alexander would rule the world. There was no hope.

Michael's heart sank. He closed his eyes and fell to his knees, defeated. It had all been for nothing.

"Have you been looking into my future again?" the thin man asked gently. "You must have seen that there is no hope. I'm sorry, my son. Do you mind if I call you that? I have no children. You're the closest thing there is on this world to someone who is like me... does that make sense? Don't you feel it, too?"

Michael loathed the thin man. He had despised him since he first saw him in a vision when he was just a little boy.

But he *did* understand. He and Joe had been inseparable, because Joe understood. Joe was like him.

"I had someone, once," Michael whispered. "His name was Joe. He was like me. He wasn't my father... not really. I said he was my grandfather, but he wasn't. He was just an old man who saw the same things I did, in the same way... He took me in after my parents died." He risked another glance at the thin man. "So yes. I do understand. When he died... it was like a part of me had passed away, too. Didn't you have anyone like that?"

The thin man shook his head in sorrow. "No. Never. I always had to find my own way. My son... you were lucky to have your Joe. I'm sorry he left you alone. But now there's another way, another chance for you to be with people who understand. Yes? You can join us."

Michael shook his head. "No."

The thin man pursed his lips. "It isn't as bad as you think it's going to be. It won't be, if you join us. You're the key, really. You could live, be happy, and make a contribution to humanity."

"Don't trust easy answers," Joe had said.

"You must accept what is, though," the thin man said.

"A man doesn't stop because he's afraid," Joe had said.

"Will you join us?"

"All men want to live in freedom," Joe had said. "It gives them hope to control their destiny, even just a little. You can hope the future will be better than today. We need that. Don't lose your hope, Michael..."

Michael just stared at him.

The thin man's face took on a thoughtful expression. "Maybe it's easier to show you. Sometimes I do this for President Peltan. I don't think you can do it, so it'll be a little bit of a shock, my son."

He reached for Michael.

As soon as his finger touched Michael's hand, the world changed.

[CHAPTER 25]

-FUTURES-

MICHAEL STOOD IN A MUSTY, PEACEFUL wood-paneled room. The thin man appeared next to him, holding his hand. "Ah. This is the palace we're going to build. Isn't it something? We'll import the wood from Earth. We're on Calvasna now. And look. There he comes."

A young man, maybe in his mid-twenties, smartly dressed in a black military uniform entered and sat at the table in the center of the room. Ian. Michael knew him instantly—he had seen him so many times before in so many futures. Several advisors and other men entered after him and sat on the opposite side of the table. One of the advisors, he realized with a shock, was himself. Older, and grown a little fatter, but definitely still Michael Forward.

He had never seen this future when he looked in

the mirror. How was that possible?

"Mr. President," one began, "The transition is a little rocky so far. There are elements in the Party who are still very loyal to President Peltan... we have moved close to many of their leaders. Just give the word."

Alexander/Ian considered. "Why should we let them live?" he asked. His voice was cold and hard. "We need to send a message."

"Perhaps," the older Michael said evenly. "But perhaps a better message would be to let them live. To round them up, but then show mercy."

Alexander/Ian seemed to consider this.

"Perhaps," he finally admitted.

Michael nodded. "Life is worth a lot, but not everything."

Time froze. Everyone stopped in place.

The thin man leaned down to whisper in Michael's ear. "In the end, he only kills about a third of them. Some of the rest of his enemies become his greatest servants. Without you there... it's much worse. Most die. By being there, you save lives!"

The scene shifted. The same room—maybe a little dimmer. Alexander/Ian still sat at the head of the table, wearing a far crueler expression.

"Mr. President," the same adviser began, "The transition is a little rocky so far. There are elements in

the Party who are still very loyal to President Peltan...
we have moved close to many of their leaders. Just give
the word."

Alexander—Michael couldn't think of him as Ian
now, not like this—nodded sharply. "I can think of no reason to keep them alive." No one else said a word. "Do
what you must. Purge them, so we can move forward."

"This," said the thin man grandly as time froze
again, "Is your impact. A better Alexander. A better man.
He'll crush his enemies. He'll kill many, yes. But far fewer
with you to guide him. He is more... humane? See here..."

The scene shifted entirely. A garden path. Alexander, younger here, spied several women strolling along,
laughing and talking, and walked up to them, grinning
like a wolf. "Ladies."

They shrank back, afraid. He pointed at one. "You.
Come with me. Now."

She burst into tears. "Please... please..."

He grabbed her and shoved her out ahead of him.
"The rest of you... later. I'll send guards."

Two men dressed in pristine white Army uniforms
advanced. They froze before they reached the women.

"You don't want to see the rest. That's without

you. But with you, he's much better. Believe me," said the thin man. "You civilize him."

The scene shifted. Michael and Alexander talked in a room somewhere. Alexander was far younger—still a child.

"I can have anything I want, can't I?" Alexander said.

Michael nodded. "Most things. But not everything."

"Father says I'll be in charge someday. That I'll be President. Then I'll have everything I want. More." He looked angry. Michael sighed and placed an arm around the youth. Alexander didn't flinch or back away.

"In fact, I think you'll have less. Being president is a terrible responsibility. Look how it ages your poor father! ... And, I want you to remember..." and here he seemed to look directly at Michael and the thin man, "Always try to be the best man you can be. *And never give up hope.*"

The thin man frowned, perplexed; had he not expected Michael to say that? Before he could collect himself, the scene shifted again. A slightly older Alexander.

"But he's a *servant*," Alexander whined. "Why shouldn't he do what I want him to?"

"Because he's also a man. A human being. Men aren't just playthings." The older Michael sighed. "I wish your foster father would realize that some days."

Alexander's eyes widened. "Like last night?"

Michael nodded. "Your father..." he stopped and thought for a moment. "All men want to live in freedom. It gives them hope..."

"Huh?" Alexander said.

The thin man looked faintly puzzled for another instant, then regained his composure.

Michael was struck with a sudden thought.

The scene shifted again.

"You see? You make him a better man. You help to shape and mold one of the greatest men who has ever lived. That's what I'm offering. That chance. And even better," the thin man said. "You'll get the chance to live."

They were in a small apartment... maybe on the palace grounds somewhere? It was hard to tell. This was the bedroom.

Michael was there, sitting on the bed. He seemed older than in the previous visions. Someone came into the room. She had black hair, streaked with gray. She wore a kind smile, but her green eyes seemed heavy and sad. "And how are you? How are things up there?"

My God. It's Monica.

Michael smiled back at her, and they touched lips lightly. "Bad. As always. You know."

Monica nodded. "Yes. I heard from Alice today.

She says that her husband is going to enlist."

"That's a terrible idea," Michael grumbled. "Going to be war soon."

"That's why, apparently." She sighed and sat next to him. "I'm so glad I at least have you close by."

He placed a hand on hers, and looked into her eyes. She smiled. "See anything?"

"You and me getting older. But together, at least."

"Well, that's a relief." She sighed and put her head on his shoulder. "I love you."

"I love you, too." He paused for a moment. "Don't lose hope. Nothing's ever broken forever."

"What?"

◆➤ ◀◆

"So you see," the thin man said hurriedly as the scene faded out. "Life. You want life. I know you do. The alternative is... hm. You know perfectly well."

The control room shimmered back into view. "You could die here. Today. You don't want to die. I know that much."

And of course, he was right. Michael didn't want to die. A small, traitorous part of him started to consider what the thin man was offering.

"What use is there in dying for something, when there's no hope at all?" the thin man asked. "You could live. You could live with your sweetheart for another fifty, sixty years. No, it won't be perfect. But what ever is? The point is, you'd be alive."

The thin man touched him again, and Michael was surrounded by beautiful, exhilarating images. Rain fell gently on his head, cool breezes blew in his face as he laughed. He looked out of a viewport at the green curve of a planet below. He kissed his wife, and took her in his arms. She was so happy. She was so beautiful. He sat and read lines from a book he loved, a warm fire crackling next to him. The sky was blue overhead. He could see for miles. For miles... life was sweet.

And then the thin man withdrew his hand and the visions disappeared. The air was hot and thick. He could hardly breathe. "All flashes of what's possible," he said. "But you won't have any of them if you continue to resist what's inevitable. So. Join us."

Michael sank back. There was nothing else he could do. It was over.

All that was left was deciding to live or die.

Life is worth a lot, but not everything. Had Joe said that?

Of course. Of course he had.

Don't give up hope.

Nothing stays broken forever.

All men want to live in freedom.

Joe had said all of that. Michael, the older Michael, had repeated them. Why?

Because, Michael thought, maybe he figured out that it wasn't worth living that life, just to be alive. Maybe he remembered this. Maybe he's warning me, trying to change the past.

But he wanted to live, to ignore the warnings and stay alive, stay breathing. So what if life wouldn't be perfect?

Nothing stays broken forever.

But there *was* no hope. There was no way out.

Nothing stays broken... Broken.

He glanced over at Broken's inert form. A spark of life returned to her glassy, open eyes as he watched.

—She flew, joyous and free, laughing and radiant as the sun's splendor... through the skies of Valen.

[CHAPTER 26]

MICHAEL CAUGHT HIS BREATH. THERE was hope. No wonder the thin man had shot her.

The thin man followed his gaze, and saw Broken start to stir. He shot her again. She went limp.

"Stop!" cried Michael. "Please!"

The thin man glared. "I'm sorry. But we can't have her coming back to life and interrupting us." He glanced over at her. "Ugh. I... *dislike* her. I *dislike* most other Extrahumans. Don't you, my son?"

Michael said nothing, praying for Broken's survival. Could she withstand this? He needed more. A very small glimmer of a plan had started to form, but he needed her back.

The thin man continued. "I mean... the power some have... it's abominable. Isn't it?"

"Sure," Michael agreed, a little dazed.

"A lot of chaos could come of them. But they won't be a problem forever, hopefully."

"You seem to get along with Sky Ranger."

The thin man smiled again. "He's a fool," he whispered. "But don't tell him so!"

Michael suddenly had a flash of inspiration, remembering his visions. "You're going to destroy Union Tower. You're going to lie about it to Sky Ranger!" he said. "Aren't you?"

The thin man's eyes narrowed. "Why do you think that?"

Michael looked at him piercingly. "I *saw* it. I see the future, remember? I saw you telling him three different things about the Tower. They were all lies, weren't they? You're going to do it yourself."

Michael suddenly remembered the archivist in Union Tower, who had been wearing Reformist pins. He'd seen the man's future. Had he been planting a bomb? "Let me guess," said Michael. "A saboteur on the inside? Someone who's been there a long time? ... The archivist? I met him. I saw some things that didn't make sense. But now..."

The thin man aimed his pistol back at Michael. "I think you had better not say anything about that. Yes. We need to get rid of them. They're dangerous. They have to die. In fact..." he checked his watch. "Ah. Ah! It should already be done. We'll blame it on terrorists. Let Sky Ranger chase them around for a while, get some exercise. It does everybody good."

"You're *evil*," said Michael, letting some of the horror he felt creep into his voice. *Come on, Broken, wake up. I need you.*

"Enough of that," snapped the thin man. "You're a fool if you believe that *evil* exists. That's something for fairy tales, isn't it? Evil villains? Men are neither good nor evil by nature. Isn't that so?"

"Men can *do* evil," Michael said, "Even when they think they are doing good."

The thin man expression turned to a scowl. His grip tightened on his weapon, trained on Michael's head. "Is that what you think? Hm. I think it's time for you to give me an answer. Join us."

Michael wanted to. God, how he wanted to. Life. Fresh air. Love. The possibilities were intoxicating.

But some things were worth so, so much more. Joe had been right.

"No," Michael said.

The thin man jabbed the laser pistol into the soft flesh of Michael's hand again. "I'm sorry. I have to convince you, my son. It's for your own good. You'll see."

He squeezed the trigger. Michael's hand exploded into flame, searing the flesh. Agony—!

He cried out, trying to clutch it, to put the fire out, something—

Before he knew it, the thin man was at his side, smothering the flames with a wet towel. Michael howled from the terrible pain, rocking back and forth on the ground. Both his hands were covered with charred skin, bones gleaming pearl-white through the blackened flesh.

"You'll get new hands," the thin man assured him. "Wonderful things, best technology available. First rate for us, yes. Don't fret. It will hurt for a while. But pain is temporary, and sometimes illuminating."

"The Union," Michael gasped. "Union Tower..."

At once the thin man rounded on him, no longer kind and soothing. "Say *nothing* of that! Not if you value your life!" He pointed the pistol at Michael's legs. "I'm warning you."

Michael sobbed quietly. The thin man sighed. "I'll wait until you're more yourself. You're coming with us. We'll work on you there. You'll come around. I believe you will, Michael, I've seen it." He tried to smile at him. "You'll forgive me someday. I've seen that, too."

The thin man left Michael curled on the floor as he busied himself with the controls scattered around the room. As the initial, searing agony ebbed, Michael's pain-fogged mind wandered to Monica. What must she be thinking? Where was she?

Would she ever escape?

"Mon... Monica," he gasped. Delirium was taking over.

"Eh?" said the thin man. "Oh. The girl. *Your* girl, or she will be. She's fine, as far as I know. Just down in a cell. Come with us, and she'll come, too. If not... well, we may let her go. I don't know yet. I'll probably have to check her out, first. She's UNP, isn't she? We may send her to a prison colony. Yes, we're starting those up, now. Cheaper than jails here, I should think. Just drop them off and your problem is solved. Very neat. She may go to one of those for a time. But she may not. I can't say. She did commit some acts of terrorism."

"Broken..." he managed to say. "Let her go..."

"Not possible," he said. "The Science Ministry so rarely gets to study Extrahumans, and I'm afraid we just blew up most of the rest of them on this planet! What a grand idea of the former regime, to put them all in one place. I wonder if they had something like this in mind. A ruthless bunch, those. Wrongheaded in so many ways. But refreshingly ruthless. The Science Ministry will study her, yes. It probably won't be very nice for her, but..."

They wouldn't let her go.

She wouldn't fly free, unless... they succeeded. He made a valiant attempt to stay conscious, to keep thinking, keep planning. He shivered violently, sick to his stomach. He focused his eyes on Broken's limp body. She had bled a lot. Did that matter to her? *Please wake up.*

"You're in shock," said the thin man. "Say the word. Give up this ridiculous quest of yours. Medical attention is just a call away. In less than an hour, the best doctors and cyberneticists on the planet will be fashioning a new pair of hands for you. What do you say? Come on, Michael. My son. Don't die for stubbornness' sake."

Broken surged upward towards consciousness. She vaguely remembered something from *last* time (whatever that was), that she had to be careful, that she mustn't make a sound. She opened her eyes carefully, just a crack, to a dreadful sight. Michael lay on the ground, and his *hands*—

She had once grabbed hold of the high electric fence surrounding Union Tower... her hands had been badly burned. She hadn't gone near the fence again, even though her hands had healed themselves quickly enough. Michael's hands wouldn't heal.

He made sounds, indistinguishable noises...

"Union Tower," he said.

"Say *nothing* of that! Not if you value your life!" The thin man aimed his pistol at Michael's legs again. "I'm warning you."

Michael dissolved into tears. The thin man was still talking, but Broken didn't hear a word.

What about Union Tower? Why did Union Tower matter? Why did the thin man care so much about it? Why couldn't Michael mention it?

At that moment, the door slid open.

Michael held his breath. He had never seen this before. He had no idea what to do. The thin man glared at him, finger ready on the trigger. All he could see was that the thin man was... terrified. He would still have no chance to speak before dying. It would be for nothing. He squeezed his eyes shut.

Bravery...

He prayed for courage.

Broken saw Sky Ranger drift through the door and take in what was going on. He cocked his head, but said nothing. How like him.

Michael wanted her to say something. She could see it in his eyes.

Broken was awake. Michael saw her staring steadily at him.

Speak, he willed her.

"Union Tower," said Broken.

The thin man wheeled, surprised, and trained his weapon on Broken.

Joe stood before him. He smiled.

"Do what you have to do," he said.

Michael fought through the pain, pushing himself upright on the stumps of his hands. His mouth formed the words.

"He destroyed Union Tower! The thin man destroyed—"

"Shut up!" cried the thin man.

He turned back to Michael. The pistol stopped its deadly arc right in front of Michael's face.

Joe beckoned.

He glanced at Broken.

She *flew*.

He was content.

The thin man pulled the trigger. Light surged into Michael's head, and his body crumpled to the ground, lifeless.

[CHAPTER 27]

THE THIN MAN TURNED ON BROKEN.

"You!" he roared, aiming at her. "I'll kill you again and again!"

She tried to move, but found her arms and legs wouldn't work.

Michael...

A black and white flash passed in front of her.

"What was that about the Tower?" said Sky Ranger to the thin man. "What happened? Why did you shoot that boy?"

The thin man sighed in agitated annoyance. "Look, Sky Ranger, better you hear from me. Well, the truth is, it's been destroyed. By, uh, terrorists. With rocket missiles. I'm sorry..."

"Lies," croaked Broken. "He did it. I heard." In fact, she dimly remembered the thin man saying so.

Sometimes hearing came back early.

"I don't believe you!" cried Sky Ranger, slapping the pistol from the thin man's grip in his rage and nearly knocking him to the ground. "I don't believe you!"

He stormed over to a screen and set it to a news channel.

"—from New York. The Union Tower fell just a few hours ago, Jeb, and it looks like it was the result of sabotage from within. Several members of the Union are suspected to have been aligned with the UNP rebels, and this may have led to—"

"My people..." Sky Ranger moaned, the color draining from his face. "My people!"

The huge man roared, and smashed a giant, white-knuckled fist into the screen. The thin man tried to edge away.

"You see? She's lying to you! We didn't do it. The terrorists did! Sky Ranger, get ahold of yourself! Now! I command you!"

Sky Ranger knelt in front of Broken. "Sil..."

"Little Hawk. Please believe me," she said. Every word was a struggle. But life flowed back into her, and she grew stronger. "Believe me. He *killed* Michael. He killed him so he couldn't tell you..."

"I don't understand..."

"You're on the wrong side," she whispered. "Crim... Crim was right. And because of that... we're the only members of the Union left alive." With a tremendous effort, she jerked her head towards the thin man. "*He* did it."

"You!" Sky Ranger advanced on him. "You *lured* me here. You wanted me *away* from my *people!* I could have *saved* so many of them—! Women and children, innocents!" Tears of anger and despair ran down his cheeks. "You—!"

"Sky Ranger!" snapped the thin man briskly. "I said it was terrorists, not us! Who are you going to believe, me or some lunatic? You don't even know her anymore!"

"Don't trust him, Sky," Broken said. "He killed Michael to shut him up."

"That was—he was going to—Sky Ranger, stop! This is a breach of—guards!"

"I trusted you! I had assurances from the highest levels that my people would be looked after!" cried Sky Ranger. He let loose a wail of pure grief and fury, and advanced on the thin man.

A flock of guards ran into the room. Sky Ranger, magnificent and terrible in his full wrath, tore them to shreds before Broken's weary eyes. His movements were a blur of black uniform and flying blood. She hadn't seen him this angry since Crimson Cadet died.

"Stop at once!" shrieked the thin man. "Please!"

He picked up his pistol and fired it at Sky Ranger. The white-hot bolts barely singed him. He was on the thin man in a flash, lifting him off the ground by both arms.

"Tell me," he growled, "Did you do it? Don't lie. I might let you live."

Broken found she could move her arms. She tried to pull herself up.

"Okay!" cried the thin man. "All right, we did! We *had* to! It was for the good of the world that Extrahumans not exist! Please, you must understand, we did what we *had* to do! What if one of you went rogue? Look at your own power! You can't be trusted, not forever, so you had to be destroyed!"

"Extrahumans are dangerous?" asked Sky Ranger, voice suddenly calm.

"Yes," confirmed the thin man.

"They should be eliminated."

"Yes," said the thin man, breathing again. "I'm glad you finally understand."

"You're an Extrahuman, too," said Sky Ranger calmly. He held the thin man by the shoulders and, with a quick, neat motion, ripped him in half. The thin man's final shriek echoed through the room.

Sky Ranger collapsed onto the hard, cold, concrete floor and sobbed hysterically.

Monica waited in the cramped cell she had been shoved into, crying softly. They'd never let her go, not now. What was happening? What had happened to the others? She thought of Wayne, Parker, Banner, and Kent... they had died without knowing what had hit them. Would they go to heaven? Did it even matter anymore? God seemed impossibly far from this place.

Where was Broken? Where was Michael? And what about poor Ian? What would become of them now?

A *whoosh* of air. Sky Ranger alighted next to the cell. She turned away in disgust. "Go away," she snapped.

"Monica," said a familiar voice. Broken. Sky Ranger carried her in his arms.

"Oh, Broken," said Monica. "You didn't...?"

"No," Broken murmured. In her arms was Ian,

asleep. Next to him were three bloodstained tickets.

"Let's go to Valen," she said.

[CHAPTER 28]

THE SUN STREAMED DOWN ON PENNY'S shoulders as she relaxed in an outdoor café not far from the Temple. She thumbed through the papers Sky Ranger had transmitted, then pushed them aside with a sigh.

Sky Ranger had stayed on Earth, even though she had implored him to come with them. What was left for him there? But he just shook his head and kissed her goodbye, his ice-blue eyes heavy. It was very like him.

He had flown them back to their hopper after they found Monica and Ian. Broken had held tightly to the baby as they careened over the endless scrubby flatlands of South Australia. Monica wept. Broken hadn't actually told her Michael was dead. She didn't need to.

His absence spoke volumes.

When they landed outside the commercial complex, military and Black Band hoppers and fighters were
circling overhead. Broken and Monica sprinted for the
safety of their waiting hopper while Sky Ranger turned
to face the oncoming attackers.

"Come with us!" cried Broken. "Sky!"

He turned to her, his handsome face a mix of fury,
desperation, and sorrow. "Go ahead, Sil. Take the kid to
Valen. Make a better future."

She ran to him. Silverwing and Silverwyng ran to
him. Broken ran to him. Penny ran to him.

"No," she sobbed. "No! Not you, too!"

He looked at her. He *really* looked at her, perhaps
for the first time.

"Oh, Sil... I'm sorry. I'm sorry about... about everything. I only wanted our people to be safe... and
now... I'm sorry. About me. About you, and about us...
I need to go make it up to everyone who's gone." His
eyes hardened, gleaming intently, something firm fixed
behind them. "I'll fight them. But it won't matter." He
deflated. "I'll fight, and eventually they'll get me."

Suddenly he brightened again. He smiled at Ian,
who was squirming in Monica's arms. "But at least I had
a hand in the future. Go on. Go. You're the last of the
Union. You have to get away."

"I loved you so much," she cried.

"I know. I'm sorry." He slipped a small disc into her
hand. "Put this on the side of the ship. They won't be
able to see you. I use one, too."

She did as she was told. He turned back to face the
circling hoppers.

"Come with us!" she begged again, desperate to convince him, not to lose him when they'd come so far.

He shook his head silently.

The attackers were getting closer. His lips met hers... and then he was soaring up into the sky. "Goodbye!" he called.

"Come on, Broken," Monica said, gently steering her into the hopper. "I'm going to try to drive this thing."

Monica clumsily lifted the ship off the ground, and guided it jerkily into the air. Silverwing—Silverwyng—Broken stared out the window, heartbroken, as Sky Ranger sped away to do battle with their pursuers.

Monica hit the thrusters, and the hopper surged forward. Ian screamed, and Broken buried her face in her hands.

◇►◄◇►

They said little on the long flight home. Monica stayed at the pilot's station, keeping the ship low over the endless sea.

The interior of the hopper seemed impossibly huge and empty, compared to the ride down. So many empty chairs... Monica could see them all, as if they were still sitting there. Michael's was the worst; she expected to see him every time she glanced at it.

About halfway to North America, she broke her silence.

"Why did Sky Ranger help us?" she asked. "I don't understand. I thought he was one of them."

"He was an Extrahuman first," Broken said sadly. "He really is a good man. He... I think he just wanted what was best for our people."

Our people. Monica had never heard her refer to Extrahumans that way before.

The hopper skimmed over the surface of the ocean as they chased the night across the planet. Only hours, now.

"Broken," she whispered. "Were you there... when... when Michael died?"

Broken nodded. "I was."

"Did you—did you see?"

She nodded again, ever so slightly.

Monica turned to Broken. Her face was lined with tears. "Did—he say anything?"

Broken shook her head. "He didn't have time to say anything."

Monica nodded to herself, turning away. "Okay. I understand." She started to shake violently. "Oh! Oh, damn him! Oh... " She burst into tears. "It was *noble,* wasn't it? That stupid—! I know him... "

Broken put a hand on her shoulder. "He died very well," she said softly. "He turned Sky Ranger against them. He knew about Union Tower, that the Reformists did it. He... he saved everything. We'd still be there if not for him. I'd be in the hands of the Science Ministry, you'd be... well, I don't know. Prison, probably, if not dead."

Monica nodded, still miserable. "I'd rather have him back!" She clung to Broken, burying her face in the woman's bloodstained cloak.

"I'd rather be dead!" she wailed. "No one's left! Everyone's gone!"

Broken held her. "I know. For me, too. Everyone's

gone..." And finally, she couldn't hold her own tears in anymore.

The Tower was gone. All of her people. Lucky. Doc. Crim. Now Sky Ranger... and Michael. So many holes had been torn in her heart, and they *ached*. Finally, she ached.

They wept together for hours as the little ship sped towards the great spaceport clinging to the edge of North America.

◄►► ◄◄►

"Don't you go anywhere," Monica murmured as dawn broke.

Broken hugged her. "Don't worry. I think I'm permanent," she said.

◄►► ◄◄►

They landed outside the approaches to Delmarva Spaceport, where Black Band-guarded trains sped emigrants to waiting interstellar ships. Broken, Monica, and Ian got on the train with no trouble; all they had to do was show their tickets to the guards.

"I wonder what will happen to the hopper?" Monica mused as the train lurched forward. "I wonder... did Wayne and Banner and the others, did they really die?"

"Yes," Broken said. "They did."

"Oh." Monica sighed. "I had been hoping I'd imagined it." She giggled, low and convulsively. "I imagine lots of things."

Broken grabbed her. "Stay with me," she commanded. "Monica. Stay with me. Don't go to that place."

Monica somehow found her control, and lay with her head in Broken's lap, silent, until the train finally pulled up outside the huge terminal complex.

◄►► ◄◄►

They stood in line for hours while government men, many of them former CA employees, checked documents, records, and tickets. Their tickets got them through most checkpoints, but when asked to produce official identification, Monica shrugged and shook her head.

"We lost it. In New York," she said. "Our house..." She looked like she might start crying again.

"I'm sorry," said the older woman in harsh, clipped tones. "I can't let you board without it. Regulations."

Such a small thing. How could they have forgotten?

"Please," said Broken quietly. "Please, we need to leave."

The old woman eyed them suspiciously. "And why would that be? Hm?"

They stood stock-still for a few seconds.

"Please," was all Monica could say. She was crying again. "Please!"

The old woman pursed her lips and shook her head. "You're holding up the line."

"You don't understand!" cried Monica. Ian wailed. The old woman heaved a long-suffering sigh and motioned to two large men, who advanced on them.

"All right, all right," Broken said, herding Monica away. "Sorry."

They slumped, devastated, in a small waiting area near the boarding gates. The next ship for Valen was leaving in an hour. There wouldn't be another for six days. The government would find them... they'd be caught, it was all for *nothing*.

"It can't end like this," Monica stammered. "It can't! Michael died so we could get away!"

Broken shook her head, looking around at the other would-be passengers. Would any of them take a baby? She had his ticket.

Probably not. She sighed. Ian still didn't have any identification. How would he get aboard? Maybe they wouldn't care if everyone else had ID. She had to try.

She stood and walked to a likely-looking woman with a kind face. "Excuse me," she said. "But this baby needs to get to Valen. We can't go. Please. Would you take him?" She handed the woman his ticket. "He should go to a nice family. *Please*."

The woman turned away. "I'm sorry," she said. "I can't."

Broken tried again and again, to no avail. Monica got up and tried people in other lines.

"I can't."

"No, I won't."

"Go away! That's illegal!"

No one wanted to speak with them. No one wanted Ian. No one wanted trouble.

A woman in a smart government uniform came up to Broken. "You need to come with me," she said. She already had Monica in tow. "Both of you. We've been monitoring you."

This was the end. They followed, sick at heart.

They had failed.

I'm sorry, Broken thought. Sky Ranger, I'm sorry. I didn't mean to fail you. Michael... Michael... you believed in us, but it looks like you were wrong. I should have known better. I'm sorry...

What a terrible ending, defeated by bureaucratic minutiae.

The woman led them into a room marked "SECURITY." Behind a large desk, surrounded by monitors, sat Janeane.

Monica's jaw dropped as the slender, dark-skinned woman rose gracefully from her chair. She wore a magnificent blue Colonization Authority uniform, in the style of the vanishing old Confederation.

"Good afternoon, ladies," she said. She smiled at the other woman. "You can go." The official saluted and left. They were alone. Janeane raised a finger and pressed a button. "Okay. No one is monitoring."

"*Janeane,*" breathed Monica, and threw herself into her arms. Janeane held her tight.

"Well. It's been a while. I thought you'd never make it."

"We did. We're here... God! I thought you'd... I thought you were... I'm so happy to see you!"

"And I you." She regarded her soberly. "I'm glad you got away. You got my note?"

Monica nodded. "Yes. Thank you. You saved my life."

Janeane laughed. "If only the others had read theirs! It figures." She shook her head. Then she looked from one to the other. "Broken, it's good to see you, too. Is Michael...?"

Broken shook her head. "Dead."

Janeane bowed her head. "May he find the sea." She gazed steadily at Monica. "I'm *glad* you left. I hoped that at least one of you would. Oh, foolish *rhin*... They always thought they'd be safe. I'm glad you're alive, honey." She kissed Monica's forehead.

Broken watched, transfixed, as the agony and grief ebbed away from Monica's face, to be replaced by the purest calm. Janeane caught her eye, and smiled a gentle, secret smile.

She is one of my people, Broken thought in wondrous envy. *And her gift is peace.*

"Thank you," said Monica, stepping back. She stood taller, no longer hunched in on herself, and seemed a dozen years younger than she had a moment before.

"And you," Janeane said, turning to Broken. "You've changed, too. I can see it."

Broken smiled and nodded, ever so slightly.

"What did you find?"

"Penny," she said softly. "It's my name. I remembered." She looked at the ground. "I think I found other things, too, but I also lost so much..."

"I know," said Janeane. "I'm proud of both of you. The child... he looks the same. But he, too, is changed. As are we all, from day to day. Well. That ship is leaving." She gave them each a sheet of paper. "Around here, what I say goes. For now, anyway. Show that to the clerk. She'll let you on."

"Will you come with us?" Monica asked.

"I can't. Not yet. But someday, I will. I promise you."

"When?"

Janeane smiled her secret little smile. "Keep an eye out for me," she said, voice warm and filled with rich promise. "By the sea."

[CHAPTER 29]

IT WORKED JUST AS JANEANE HAD SAID.
They got to the head of the line again, and showed the irritable clerk the piece of paper. Reading it, she smiled graciously and issued them boarding passes, instructing them to run to make the ship; they got to the ship just as boarding was ending.

They found berths easily—ships to the lesser colonies never filled up—and crowded next to the window to watch as the cavernous vessel strained and groaned, slowly lifting itself off the oceans of concrete that encased the Delmarva Peninsula, and thrusting up into the night sky. Monica held Ian tightly, and sat pressed back against the seat, eyes squeezed shut. Broken watched as the concrete receded, then was surrounded by water. The continent gradually revealed itself as they strove ever higher. Soon the curve of the Earth was visible, and, as the starship picked up speed, the blue-green sphere of the planet gradually fell away.

They left New York and the ruins of Union Tower behind. They left Yonkers and the remains of Monica's family's house. They left New Jersey and the whole of shattered, forgotten America, too.

Michael was down there. Had he been moved? Would they bury him? Or would he remain in that control room, eternal witness to his triumph, forever? It didn't matter to him, not anymore.

Had he seen it? Had he known what was coming? Probably, Broken reasoned. And what did that say?

Sky Ranger was still there. Broken ached for the man she'd lost, then so recently discovered anew. He would stay until he succeeded or died. He would almost certainly not succeed.

The ship groaned again, and Broken and Monica clutched Ian as they shuddered and sped off into hyperspace. The universe seemed to *shift*—and then nothing at all was visible out of the porthole. Earth was behind them; the colony world of Valen ahead.

The trip took more than two months. Broken and Monica spent the first few days locked in their tiny cabin, but soon, out of sheer boredom, they ventured out into the common areas of the ship.

On the fifth day, they sat in a vast, curving lounge, away from the other passengers. Ian slept fitfully in Monica's arms. She hadn't let him out of her sight since they took off. From time to time, she broke the silence by singing nonsense songs to him. He didn't seem to like them, and cried sometimes when she started to sing and bounce him awkwardly.

"Michael was so good with him," Monica said. "How did he do that?"

Michael hadn't been good with Ian at all, Broken reflected. But there was no way to say that to Monica, whose face had lit up into a smile for the first time since Australia.

"Michael would have been a great father, don't you think?" She sighed wistfully. "He really would have been."

Broken turned away. She couldn't bring herself to think about Michael any longer. Ian gurgled in his sleep.

Doc administered the shot quickly, gracefully, and painlessly. "There. No problem. And we got it done before you had a chance to heal around it! Not an easy task, Silly-girl." His old nickname for her.

Silverwing rubbed her arm absently, watching the wound close up. "How long is this good for?"

"A year. You get another next June."

"Does everyone get one?"

Doc nodded. "Everyone in the Tower, from when you turn eleven. Just to be on the safe side. Didn't they tell you about this in Health Studies?"

Sil shrugged. "Maybe."

"It's to keep you from having a baby. You know how babies are made, right?"

She nodded soberly. There had been a video on the subject.

"All right, then."

"What if I want to have a baby?" Silverwing asked. She hadn't ever really considered having one, but maybe someday she would.

Doc shook his head. "You can't. That's the law. We aren't allowed."

"Oh," Sil said. Her face fell. "Why?"

"Because," Doc said. "How's that arm doing?"

"Fine," she said.

"Okay. I have other people to see, so get a move on. I'll see you next week for a checkup, right?"

She nodded.

"All right, then. Off you go."

Sky Ranger would have been a horrible father, she realized. Broken sneaked a look at Ian, who had fallen back to sleep after an hour of nonstop wailing. She probably wouldn't have been a great mother, either. But, as with so many things in her life, it would have been nice to have had the choice.

Michael, whose life seemed to run on rails, hadn't really had choices, either. Or had he? He must have known what was going to happen to him, right? She didn't say this to Monica, but kept it to herself, guarding it like a jewel, holding it close to her heart.

He knew. He knew all his possibilities ended in a dark room with a man and a gun. But he went to Australia anyway.

Monica and Broken spoke little of the past, but more of their hopes for the future.

"Valen will have fewer Black Bands," Monica said. "Don't you think? I heard some of the other passengers talking about that."

"Maybe," Broken said thoughtfully. "It would be nice."

"We can live there without being afraid. That's why a lot of people are on this trip. To get away."

"Mm," Broken murmured, smiling. "What do you want to do once you're there?"

"I... don't know. Maybe go back to school? There are colleges on Valen, right?"

"I have no idea."

Monica had heard of the Blues, a religious group who followed the wisdom of the prophet Valentino Al-trera. He was the one for whom Valen had been named.

"I followed one prophet, I can follow another," Monica announced. "I want to at least go to the Great Temple in Arve."

Broken agreed to this. Arve was Valen's capital and only major city. They would land near there. Other than that, they were coming to realize they knew next to nothing about their destination.

"I've also heard they help people who need it," Monica said quietly. "Maybe they can help us, too."

Both of them looked at Ian, snoozing in Monica's arms. They still hadn't talked about what they were going to do with him once they arrived.

The future seemed much wilder and more unknowable than ever. Not for the first time, Broken wished she had Michael back, so he could explain it to her.

Ian grew a little bigger, and started crawling aggressively all over the ship. The other passengers got used to the sight of him, scooting along happily while either Monica or Broken chased him.

One day, Broken stopped Monica as she was going to take a shower.

"Monica," she said. "I want to be Penny from now on. Okay?"

Monica smiled. "Of course. Penny. I like that name. It's very pretty."

Penny nodded thoughtfully. "It doesn't suit me. But it's *mine*."

They saw Valen for the first time as a small blue globe hanging tantalizingly in front of the forward viewport. Passengers yelled and cheered. Valen was like a blue beacon of freedom for all of them. Here, the heavy hand of Peltan's Confederation would not be so keenly felt—at least not for a little while, yet. Penny didn't need to see the future to know that it wouldn't last.

But for now, they were safe.

[CHAPTER 30]

THE STARSHIP, TO THEIR SURPRISE, did not land. Instead, they docked at an orbital station, where shuttles waited patiently to take them to Arve. It was explained that no one on Valen wanted to create a concrete sea like Delmarva. Penny and Monica, gazing on the pristine blue-white beauty of the planet below, had to agree.

A cheerful, talkative man ferried them down to the surface in his four-seater. On the way, he told them about his home in the hills outside Arve, and how glad he was he had come from Ohio to here.

"No comparison," he said several times. "No way. This place is great. Some weird people, religious stuff, but mostly people leave each other be. You'll see. It's great!"

They landed at a small spaceport outside the city.

When Penny first stepped out of the spacecraft and onto Valen's surface, she was surprised at how light she felt. The gravity here was a little less than Earth's. She breathed in. The air smelled sweet, fresh. The sky was a somewhat different shade of blue, though. She'd have to get used to that.

Arve was a motley collection of temporary-looking prefabricated structures mixed in with the occasional more permanent stone or brick building. The streets were laid out in an orderly grid, although many of the blocks were still entirely empty. The city was new and bright, and people seemed happy and optimistic wherever they went. Every once in a while, they encountered men and women dressed entirely in blue walking the streets, talking to people. The Blues, Penny guessed; the followers of Val Altrera.

They walked into the city, taking turns carrying Ian. They saw no Confederation military or Black Bands anywhere. They learned later that while some on Valen supported Peltan, the Reformist militia didn't exist here. The Valenane thought them bizarre.

They made their way to a large temple in the western quarter of Arve, and knocked on a door set apart from the main entrance, without knowing why. An old man dressed in a blue robe opened it.

His face lit up when he saw Ian. "Well, little man!" he said. "Well!" He noticed Penny and Monica. "What can I do for you two?"

"We—" Penny began, but Monica cut her off.

"Sanctuary," she said. "Please."

The man nodded. "You are welcome. Just come from Earth?"

<=> <=>

The keepers of the Blue Order, the ones who followed Val Altrera, took them in, as Monica had hoped. Many other immigrants had come to West Arve Temple, as well. The monks here took their duties seriously, and helped as many as they could.

As time passed, they started seeing Black Bands and Reformist signs in the streets, sometimes, but still far, far fewer than at home. Here on Valen, Earth and its politics were very distant.

Life at the temple took on a peaceful rhythm. They awoke with the men and woman of the Order at dawn, said a quick morning prayer of thanks and asked for strength and wisdom to complete the day's tasks. Then Penny and Monica helped do chores like watering and ridding the gardens of the—strange purplish weeds that threatened the delicate Earth transplants— sweeping the wood and stone floors, and tending to the sick, infirm, and elderly refugees who stayed in the massive temple complex. Then lunch, and other chores or, if there was nothing else to do, time to explore what there was of the city.

Penny found that she liked evenings best, though, when the entire temple community gathered to sing, chat, and pray. It was peaceful, and the monks made a point of making everyone gathered there feel welcome. Even though Penny didn't necessarily believe in all of the words the monks said, she still felt, for the first time in a long time, that she belonged somewhere.

Monica seemed to feel the same. She started to follow the monks around, and began to learn all that they could teach her. Her hair had faded from the dyed black it had been, and was now a serene, deep brown. Her green eyes were still sad and heavy, but now there was a calmness Penny hadn't expected. These days, every once in a while, she even cracked that old, crooked smile of hers.

Dumont, the old man who had first opened the door for them, an assistant to the prelate, commented to Penny that at the rate she was going, Monica might soon "take the Blue." That seemed to happen to a certain slice of the refugees, he told her. Something about the peace and stability of temple life appealed to them. He gave Penny a meaningful look as he said it, but she deflected him with a smile.

Then, one day, a package arrived at the temple.

"Excuse me," said a young novice, coming up to some of the immigrants while they were doing their chores. "But are any of you named 'Silver Wing,' by any chance?" Penny hesitantly raised a hand. "Something's come for you from Earth."

Monica had been out all week, walking the local routes with one of the itinerant monks to see what the life of a Blue was like. Penny took the sheaf of paper that had come in a disarmingly normal ConFedPost box and read it hungrily—then wished she hadn't.

She took herself to a nearby café, where she bought a hot chocolate with the money she'd earned by washing the clothes of other immigrants —she thought about a drink, but she hadn't had one in ages and she didn't want to start again.

She read over the first page again.

"Silverwyng," it began. "I found these in a Black Bands headquarters in New York. I think you'll find them interesting. The situation here is very bad. I won't be able to hold out for much longer. Please keep this safe. Please remind the world that we existed, once. Good-bye. Sky."

So quick and simple. How very Sky Ranger. She sighed and flipped through the documents again.

Records, detailing every occupant the Tower had ever held. Plans to the building. Government progress reports. Scientific data, theories about why and how Extrahumans existed. And, worst, a military document from twenty years before, cataloging all the ways that Union Tower could be destroyed in the event of an "emergency." Penny shook her head sadly, but she wasn't surprised.

The government was different now, but in one respect UNP and Reform were the same: They both wanted to destroy what lived in Union Tower. The Extrahumans were, as the papers noted time and again, a threat. The old government had held them prisoner, kept them from having children, and sent their best and strongest out to capture those Extrahumans who had dared to live free. The new government had been much more direct, but they shared the same objective: the end of the Extrahuman race.

She kept remembering Sky Ranger's face as the reality of Union Tower's destruction sank in. *My people*, he had said. At that moment, she had realized it was true. Her people, unique in the universe. People like Michael,

Sky Ranger, Crimson Cadet, Lucky Jane... Her people... who were now gone. So many, gone.

There was a rustle of robes. She looked up to find a short, severe-looking woman with a downturned mouth approaching.

"Prelate!" she exclaimed, surprised. The seldom-seen prelate of the temple, a woman named Celeste, smiled thinly down at her.

"May I sit?" she asked. She nodded, and the woman slid into a chair. "Oooh, my poor back."

For an instant, Penny considered hiding the papers, then thought better of it. "Prelate," she said softly, handing them to her. "Please... take these. Can you keep them safe?"

She nodded. "I can. Are they important?"

"Yes," she said, looking down. "They're a record. Of my people."

"Extrahumans?" the prelate asked softly. Penny glanced up sharply. "Come," the woman said. "I saw you cut your finger in the garden, and have it heal a moment later. You must be one of the only ones left. I'm very sorry."

Penny shrugged. What was there to say?

"I will take them, if you want. We have an archive at Clearfield. Would you like a copy for yourself?"

"I would," she said. "Thank you."

She ordered a tea. "Your friend Monica is becoming well versed in the lessons St. Val taught us," the prelate said. "She seems much more content, now. However, she still doesn't like talking about her past."

"It was—hard," Penny replied.

"I know," she said. "I can tell from your faces. But

the child...? That is what concerns me most."

"I don't know," Penny said. "I... I don't think I can keep him. He's supposed to go to someone else."

"Oh?" The normally sober and reserved prelate suddenly seemed like a child with a great secret, bouncy and bursting.

"He's... important," Penny said. "Really. Or, at least, someone I once knew thought so. But he thought a lot of things that didn't turn out to be true."

"Such as?"

She sighed bitterly. "He said I would fly again."

Prelate Celeste's eyes lit up. "I knew it," she said to herself. "Damn St. Val for being so vague! Here, take this!" She withdrew an envelope from the folds of her robes. "We've been waiting a long time for you! Yes, we knew you'd come, the woman who could heal herself in an instant, but had forgotten how to fly, with the child. It's the first step down a long path. We had hoped—but here." She pressed the paper into Penny's waiting hand.

"What—?"

"Valentino Altrera, who founded our order, was like your friend," the prelate said. "He could see the future, too. He knew the possibilities. He knew you'd come! He knew what to do, and before he died, he told me to give you these instructions."

Penny's skin prickled.

"Now go get that boy," Celeste ordered archly, "And take him to where he is supposed to be!"

Penny jumped up and sprinted out of the café.

◆◈▸ ◂◈▸

She carried him high into the hills surrounding Arve. Ian laughed and giggled as Penny struggled under his weight, his curls tickling her nose as he squirmed— he had finally grown a real head of hair. He had grown so heavy, too! He could walk now, but only a few tottering steps at a time.

The air up here was colder, and the view magnificent. She walked along a twisting, winding road up the side of one mountain and down another. Great, green fields, filled with crops both alien and familiar, grew here. A beautiful place.

She stopped, checking the address on the piece of paper the prelate had given her. Here, yes. She walked down the lane to a house, and knocked on the door. The name on the plate read "DELARIAN."

A grizzled man of maybe forty opened the door. "Yeah?" he asked. He looked like the sort of man who had seen a lot in his time. He hadn't shaved in days.

Penny held out Ian to him. "He is for you," she said simply. "He belongs here."

For a moment, she was afraid he would tell her to go away. But he didn't. His face thawed, then broke open in joy as he realized she said nothing but the truth. Ian locked eyes with the man, and smiled serenely.

Penny left him there, and walked alone down the dusty road. Now what would she do?

"I've done it, Michael!" she called to the open air. "I've done it!" She laughed, but the sound was hollow. "I've done it. I have." But what would she do now? What was left?

As she walked, drained and dejected, towards the city, a strange feeling came over her. Her body lightened and loosened, until she felt that she weighed nothing at all, that her legs and arms were made of sunlight.

She inhaled, tasting the fresh, sweet air, then stretched out her arms and jumped, leaping high into the air. In a flash of perfect awareness, everything flooded back to her. She shrieked and whooped with joy as she flew into the bright and sunny skies of Valen.

[EPILOGUE]

To be opened by Penny Silverwing
July 21st, 2107

Hello, Penny,
Michael Forward and others have told you about
me. Thank you for everything that you've done, and for
all that you've sacrificed.
I have included an address on the other side of
this paper. Take the boy there. A good man waits to
raise him as his son. Should he grow up, the human
race will be better for it

You will hear from me again, but for now, fly, and
live. The skies of this world are clear and blue, and a
bright soul like you belongs in them.

VAL

Valentino Altrera
West Arve, Valen, Terran Confederation
August 5th, 2101

Susan Jane Bigelow is a native New Englander
and librarian with a passion for books,
computers, and writing.

She lives in northern Connecticut
with her wife and cats.

Broken is her first novel.

Keep up with the author online:
http://susanjanebigelow.wordpress.com/
Twitter: @whateversusan

FLY
INTO
FIRE
Susan Jane Bigelow

**If you enjoyed *Broken*, be sure to check out
Fly Into Fire, the second novel in the
Extrahumans series!**

The last Sky Ranger of the now-vanished Extrahuman Union, defeated by his former allies and detested by everyone else, had fled Earth and the repressive Confederation in a desperate attempt to put the past to rest. But when his refugee ship crashes on a desert planet, his life is thrown back into chaos, and his future becomes less certain than ever. There he meets abrasive, impulsive Renna, and Dee, a flighty, secretive orphan girl, who are the only two refugees who can stand him.

When Dee wanders off into the wilderness, Sky Ranger chases after her, touching off a series of events that lead them and their companions from the deserts of Seera Terron through alien Räton space and to the very heart of the Confederation itself. Sky Ranger must confront his past and a intrusive, ruthless government if he wants to be able to save her and his people from utter destruction.

Fly Into Fire, the follow-up to the critically acclaimed **Broken**, is a story of hope, adventure, friendship and sacrifice, in a world when only freedom to be found is within.

CPSIA information can be obtained at www.ICGtesting.com
Printed in the USA
LVOW101749061211

258108LV00007B/40/P